MOTOWN and DIDI

ALSO BY WALTER DEAN MYERS

The Nicholas Factor
Won't Know Till I Get There
The Black Pearl & The Ghost
Fast Sam, Cool Clyde, and Stuff
The Golden Serpent
It Ain't All for Nothin'
The Legend of Tarik
Mojo and the Russians
The Young Landlords

MOTOWN and DIDI

A Love Story

BY WALTER DEAN MYERS

VIKING KESTREL

VIKING
A Division of Penguin Books USA Inc., 375 Hudson Street, New York, New York, 10014
Penguin Books Ltd, 27 Wrights Lane, London W8 5TZ (Publishing & Editorial) and
Harmondsworth, Middlesex, England (Distribution & Warehouse)
Penguin Books Australia Ltd, Ringwood, Victoria, Australia
Penguin Books Canada Limited, 2801 John Street, Markham, Ontario, Canada L3R 1B4
Penguin Books (N.Z.) Ltd, 182-190 Wairau Road, Auckland 10, New Zealand

First published in 1984 by Viking Penguin Inc.
Published simultaneously in Canada
Printed in the United States of America
by R. R. Donnelley & Sons Company
Set in Sabon
10 9 8 7 6 5

Library of Congress Cataloging in Publication Data
Myers, Walter Dean.   Motown and Didi.
Summary: Motown and Didi, two teenage loners in Harlem, become allies in
a fight against Touchy, the drug dealer whose dope is destroying Didi's
brother, and find themselves falling in love with each other.
[1. Harlem (New York, N.Y.)—Fiction. [2. Afro-Americans—Fiction.
3. Drug abuse—Fiction] I. Title.
PZ7.M992Mot 1984 [Fic] 84-3632 ISBN 0-670-49062-8

MOTOWN and DIDI

MOBY DICK

CHAPTER   I

MOTOWN HADN'T ALWAYS LIVED IN ABANDONED BUILD-
ings, and he hadn't always lived on 135th Street. But he
had been living in old buildings for four years, and on
135th Street for almost a full year now. Not that 135th
and Lenox was so great. Two years earlier a fire had gutted
several buildings on the block, and the city had sent a
construction firm up to Harlem to finish the job. They said
it was for the safety of the other residents, so that the
buildings wouldn't collapse and injure anyone. They left
an empty lot where people would come and dump their
garbage. In the winter winos built fires there in trash cans
to keep away the cold. The building Motown was living
in had emptied out soon after the fire. The building next
to him was also vacant. At first its windows had been
covered just with galvanized tin; then the city had put
pictures of windows over the tin, to make it look as if
people were still living in the building.

The junkies had come in and taken out all of the plumb-
ing. Lead pipes went for four cents a pound if they were
clean, two cents a pound if they were painted. The first
floor, because it was closest to the garbage in the empty
lot, was where the rats lived. Motown lived on the third
floor.

When he woke the first Monday after losing a job at

Empire State Carriers, it was raining. That was a good sign. A lot of people might stay home and miss some job that he, going out in the rain, could then get. He lay on the small cot by the window in Apartment #4, overlooking Lenox Avenue itself, and mapped out his plan of action. He would look two days for a good job. The other three days he would take anything, no matter how temporary, to make ends meet. He didn't mind what kind of work he had to do, as long as it was honest.

He got up, checked his bag to make sure that all of his toilet articles were there, dressed, and went downstairs. On the first floor he watched as two rats scampered along the floor, then ran up a wall and into the hole where the mailbox had been before the building had been condemned. He went to the door, looked out carefully to make sure that no one was around, and then slipped out into the rainy morning. It didn't do to let people see you come and go. Winos or junkies might think you had a few dollars stashed away in your place and then tear it up searching for it; or, not finding anything, they might burn up your bedding or leave their wastes on it in anger.

Motown had his stash, four hundred dollars, in a bank downtown. He kept his bankbook in a belt that he wore under his clothes. He had made the belt by cutting and sewing up an old army jacket he'd found. He had put buttons on it so he could fasten it around his waist.

"Hey, Motown, where you goin' so early?" Tutmose Rogers wiped at the sweat which ran down the side of his head.

"Downtown to see if I can find me a job," Motown said.

"That piece of job I had down in the garment center didn't last like the guy said it would."

"Yeah, I know what you mean," Tutmose said. "You want a paper?"

Motown took one of the papers that Tutmose was selling, reached into his pocket for the change to pay for it, then saw Tutmose's hand go up. "You ain't gonna make no money giving your papers away, Tutmose," he said.

"Go on, Motown," Tutmose said, grinning. "You know me and you tight."

Motown started toward the subway. It made him feel good to walk with all the other people getting out in the morning. What made a difference between people was what you did in the morning. If you got up and went out to work you were one kind of person; if you didn't have anywhere to go you were a different kind. Motown was seventeen, almost eighteen, and most of the people he knew around his age didn't have anything more to do than hang out in the streets. There wasn't anything wrong with the streets—just that Motown sometimes thought they weren't the real world. Sometimes, too, he thought that some of the people he saw in the streets weren't the real people.

"You see them young men walking down these streets," the Professor would say, sitting in front of his bookshop on Lenox Avenue. "They aren't just youngbloods, they're warriors walking along the edges of their tribal lands, exalting their manhood."

It sounded good, Motown thought, young black warriors protecting their lands, but it didn't always seem like it.

Motown went down into the subway at 125th Street and got on line to buy a token.

"How much the tokens cost?" a heavyset woman in front of him turned around and asked.

"Ninety cents," Motown said.

"I ain't got no ninety cents," she said. "I need fifteen cents. How much you got?"

"I ain't got no fifteen cents to be giving you," Motown said.

"Why you be so mean?" the woman asked. "You a nice-looking guy and everything. I got to get downtown and see about a job."

Motown looked at the coins in his hand and gave the woman fifteen cents.

"Where you live?" she asked. "If I see you around I'll give you the fifteen cents."

"That's okay," Motown said.

"Where you live?" she asked again, as they both went through the turnstiles.

"A Hundred Thirty-fifth Street," Motown· said.

"That's a nice block," the woman said. The train squealed noisily as it came into the station and ground to a screeching halt. "My name's Johnnie Mae. What's yours?"

"Motown."

"If I ever see you up on a Hundred Thirty-fifth Street I'll give you your fifteen cents," she called out. Motown watched as she went through the doors and cut across the subway car just in time to beat a man dressed in a business suit to a seat. She looked up at Motown and winked.

He didn't know if he should go to Fourteenth Street or

to Warren Street to look for a job. Warren Street sometimes had messenger jobs, which were better than the loading and unloading jobs or the garment center jobs you could get from Fourteenth Street. But there were more agencies on Fourteenth Street and the chances of getting a job were better, so he decided to go there.

At the Sterling Agency on Fourteenth he was told that there were two jobs available: one on Eighth Avenue and one down on Church Street. Both paid the same, three dollars and fifty cents an hour.

"The messenger job," Motown said, "you go around on foot?"

"They give you a bicycle," was the answer, "but the owner says you can get tips."

"What's the one on Church Street doing?" Motown asked.

"It's working at one of those discount places. The guy just said he needed somebody. He don't need no experience."

Motown took the job on Church Street. He had seen too many guys get hit by cars as they zigzagged on bicycles through midtown traffic. He had even tried it once and hadn't been able to sleep at nights, thinking about what he would face the next day.

The guy at Church Street looked like an Arab. He spoke softly, telling Motown that what he had to do was to keep the selling floor clean. That was okay, and Motown put in eight hours.

"I don't think I'll need you tomorrow," the Arab said. Motown never quite got his name, but it sounded something like Cat-Hob. "But give me a call Wednesday and I'll tell you if I need you again."

"If you don't need somebody, why you say you do?" Motown asked. "I had to give the man twenty-five dollars for this job."

"You're a good worker," the Arab said. "Let me talk to my brother."

Motown sat down on a box and waited while the Arab went and spoke to his brother. He wasn't tired from the work even though he had been busy all day, making sure that the floor was clean, emptying the trash cans, and occasionally moving packages for the sales people. But not having a job at the end of the day made him tired. He was tired of looking around all the time and even more tired of ending up in the same place from where he had started.

"My brother says he is sorry," the Arab said, returning. "But the boy we used to have is coming back tomorrow. I'll give you the twenty-five dollars you paid for the job and you leave with me your telephone number. If I need somebody again, I will call you."

Motown made up a telephone number and gave it to the Arab. The Arab, as he had promised, gave Motown the twenty-five dollars he had paid for the job.

Maybe, Motown thought, the guy at the jobs place would give him another job for nothing since this one had lasted only one day, and then the twenty-five dollars would be all profit. Maybe.

The Lexington Avenue train was older than most of the other subway lines. It rocked and protested shrilly as it made its way uptown. Motown leaned against the doors and thought about the Arab brothers who owned the store on Church Street. He wondered where they had come from and what they had been like at his age. Then he switched his mind to his plan for the week. Would he spend two more days looking for a steady job, now that this one had faded after one day, or would he look for just one more day? If he looked for two more days and didn't find anything, he could sell some blood for nine dollars to make up the day.

He got off at 125th Street so he could walk the rest of the way home. He liked this time of day in Harlem. People would pour off the train at 125th and spread quickly through the streets in a hundred directions to their homes and families.

When he was in the mood Motown could sense the life that steamed from the concrete walks. And when he did, he would smell the odors of life, new and old, that pushed out from the red brick tenements and hung like ivy from the fire escapes. Like some people could feel a change in the weather, Motown could feel changes in the streets. Sometimes, on those mornings following the sleepless nights that came all too often, he wished that it weren't so.

But wishing didn't make anything change. Maybe later, when he had his own place, things would change. Sometimes he thought about how it would be to sit at his own window and look down at the street. His own window, squaring off a patch of space that was his. It would be good.

He slowed down as he reached his corner. If anyone was hanging around in front of the building he lived in, he wouldn't go near it. He would walk someplace else, waiting until the coast was clear, until the shadows had gathered over the streets and sent the wine drinkers to their corner posts, and pushed the people off the streets into their apartments. Then he would go to the place he was calling home. He turned the corner slowly, pretending that the signs in the window of the bodega interested him. Out of the corner of his eye he saw something going on. There was a group of people, some dudes around a girl he had seen around the block. He thought her name was Didi.

It wasn't everything. That was what Darlene Johnson had fixed her mouth to say. It wasn't everything, because the sun kept burning and the earth kept turning—that's what she was fixing her mouth to say. But then she saw her daughter's face in the mirror, saw the pain and hurt twisting Didi's brown face into an ugly mask, and she didn't let the words come out as she had planned them.

"Why you got to go away to school anyhow?" Darlene asked, as she picked out her hair. "There's plenty of colleges right here in New York."

"What kind of money do I have to go to college without a scholarship?" Didi asked.

Then she stood, her back against the old cast-iron sink, and listened to her mother talking about how Didi could find a job and go to school at night, and how Mrs. Dodson had told her that, and how it would be better than going off to some school way out in Washington.

"Why in the world you want to go to school way out in . . . you know, that's clear on the other side of the country?" her mother asked. "You know that?"

I know it, Didi thought to herself. She just turned and went into the room she shared with her mother, looking back once to see her mother resume picking out her hair in front of the mirror, which was propped against a box of salt on the table.

What had Mrs. Greene said in school? Oh, yes, something about if it were back in the seventies, they would have given her a scholarship easily because they were looking for blacks then.

"I have a ninety-two average!" Didi had said. "Ninety-two!"

"If you had done better on the SATs, maybe." Mrs. Greene shook her head. "You know they weigh everything."

Weigh everything? They hadn't weighed the night before Didi had taken the SAT. They hadn't weighed her mother saying she was going to run to the store and then not coming back home until almost daybreak. They hadn't weighed Didi's walking around the neighborhood all night looking for her mother as she had done years ago, when she was ten and Tony was only nine. Then they had found their mother sitting on the curb talking to herself and some men laughing and making fun of her. When she and Tony had managed to get her home, Didi had had to stay home from school with her for a week, to make sure that she didn't wander away again.

Mrs. Lucas, the nosy old lady on the first floor, said that her mother wasn't "right." She said that it was a shame that Didi and Tony were still in her care. She told this to

Didi, too, as if Didi wanted to hear it, as if Didi had wanted to stand in the hallway, one thin brown leg twined around the other, and listen as this woman said that her mother should be "put away" somewhere for her own good.

"Yes, ma'am," Didi had said, politely. She knew it was better just to let people say what they had to say if you were a child; that way they didn't get upset.

She could have told Mrs. Lucas that her mother had once been away someplace for a year, while she and Tony lived with their cousin in Queens. She could have told her that Tony used to cry and wet the bed and then get beaten for it. And they would dream about their mother coming home, looking like a brown Snow White or maybe somebody from the cover of *Ebony*, and taking them away to a beautiful place.

The night before the SATs, Darlene hadn't come back until dawn. There was the smell of liquor on her breath, though Didi knew that her mother didn't drink to speak of.

"You okay, Mama?" Didi took her mother's face in her hands and looked into the soft brown eyes, now oddly distant. "You okay?"

"I'm tired, Didi," she had said.

Didi helped her into the bedroom and watched as she lay heavily across the bed.

"Take your clothes off, Mama," Didi said.

Her mother didn't move. Didi pulled the blanket from beneath her and then covered her with it gently.

Most of the time it was all right, though. It was just that once in a while, like an occasional eclipse of the moon, her mother seemed to disappear from among them in all but body. She would be strange then, another person, a woman that Didi could scarcely recognize. Sometimes Darlene would wander away for hours or days at a time, and sometimes she would hurt herself, walking into walls, falling lifelessly over the least obstacle.

But always she was a woman, and it was this which made her even the more vulnerable and which alerted Didi to her own womanhood.

"It's not everything, baby," her mother had said when Didi received the letter from Eastern Washington University saying that they were sorry that they could not offer her a full scholarship, but that some tuition aid was available.

"Why you want to go all the way to the other side of the *country?*" Darlene had asked her daughter, emphasizing the word country to add weight to it.

Didi hadn't answered her mother. Yes, she realized it was all the way on the other side of the United States. Wasn't that why she had picked it? She wanted to go there and bury herself in the books that would make her forget who she was and where she came from. She had been home too long, with her mother too long, holding those fragile hands when things went wrong, the thin fingers, the veins twisting like sycamore roots up the arms. Was she the daughter? The child? Perhaps there had been a mistake, and it wasn't Darlene that wasn't "right" but Didi, and she was really the mother.

The day before the SATs she had thought about the tests a great deal, about how hard she had studied for them.

She dreamed that she would score so well that colleges across the country would offer her full scholarships. Perhaps she would go to one of the Ivy League schools. She would only be seventeen when she graduated, too. They would be impressed by that.

"Miss Johnson . . ." A tall white man, utterly distinguished looking, would be speaking to her from behind an enormous mahogany desk. "I can't remember when we've seen such a high score on the Scholastic Aptitude Tests. We're sure you'll do just fine in college, and we'd like to offer you a full scholarship plus money for your expenses here at Vassar."

She had searched the streets until two in the morning and then went home. Tony was there, and she woke him up and told him that their mother had wandered off.

"When she go?" Tony asked, not sitting up in bed.

"About seven," Didi said. "She said she was just going to the store on the corner."

"She'll be back," Tony said. "You call the police or anything like that?"

"You think I should?"

"What they gonna do?" Tony turned his back to her.

She did come back, though. About four-thirty Mr. Lee knocked on the door and told Didi that her mother was downstairs in the hallway.

"I think she might have messed herself up a little," he said, embarrassed.

Didi went downstairs and brought her mother up, thankful that she seemed okay, fearful of what might have happened to her during the night, fearful of the kind of people she had met.

In the house she checked to see that her mother's keys were still in her bag. They were, but her money was gone. Didi got her mother cleaned up and into bed.

Didi's eyes were red from fatigue and crying, but she drifted off to sleep in a chair. When the alarm went off it startled her. She looked at the time. Six-thirty. She turned the alarm off and went to the bathroom and washed up. The SATs weren't until nine, but she didn't dare lie down, lest she sleep through the time to go. She made instant coffee and waited until almost seven-thirty before she woke Tony.

"No way," Tony said. "I got to take care of some business today."

"What's more business than your mother?" Didi asked. "Somebody has to be around today, in case she goes out or something. You know that."

"So stay around," Tony said. He got out of bed. There was a hole in the back of his shorts. Didi made herself a mental note to sew it.

"I have to take the SATs today," Didi said. "If I don't take them today I can't take them until the summer, and then it's too late to apply for scholarships."

"So what you want from me?" Tony's voice, muffled, came through the bathroom door. There was the sound of running water.

"So stay with her!"

"Yeah, okay."

Lie. He was lying, Didi knew he was lying. He would

go out with his friends. He would put on his clothes and then go down and hang around The Starlight. She started to ask him to swear, but she knew that it wouldn't do any good; he would swear and it wouldn't have any meaning.

She went into where her mother lay diagonally across the bed. Her leg had come out from under the cover. It was long and brown and shapely. Her mother was a good-looking woman. Images flashed in Didi's mind about what could have happened to Darlene Johnson during the night. She took them with her to the SATs.

Darlene Johnson did day's work when she could find it and collected welfare when she couldn't. She hated welfare. She hated taking anything from anybody. Her father, a Holiness minister who had died from diabetes, used to tell her that a man that had his hand out begging was less than a dog. When Darlene's husband left her, she didn't send anybody looking for him. He announced that he was leaving one morning, talking about how he needed more room to find himself as a man and whatnot. She had known he was going to leave. She had seen the signs, the little arguments, the staying out late, him slicking his hair back before he went out. She had seen the signs. That's why she wasn't surprised when he started packing his things.

"You can't find yourself as no man because you ain't got that much man in you," she said, hoping that she could hurt him just half as much as he was crushing her.

He left that morning, and she went and found a job that afternoon. She had often told the story to Didi and Tony, knowing she should have said something kind about the hazel-eyed fool who had left her with two nothing-more-than-babies and a chill that blankets couldn't come close to cutting. Tony seemed to be like his father, didn't want to do nothing much more than be cute, but Didi was okay. Smart, too. Got a job after school and wasn't a burden at all.

Tony was into a fast crowd, and he and Didi had had a fight about bringing them to the house.

"I don't want them people in my house," Didi had said. "They're smoking reefer and you know it. First thing I know, you're going to have one of them things in your mouth."

"Now, what I look like smoking reefer?" Tony glanced over toward his mother. "I ain't no fool."

Yes, you are, Didi said to herself. She knew that Tony was fooling around with marijuana. She had come home and smelled it in the house when his friends were there. Another time she had found a part of a reefer in an ashtray.

She didn't like it, but she had always told herself that it wasn't the worse thing in the world. She had seen the others on the street, the junkies, leaning against the buildings or nodding out on the stoop, doing their slow-motion death dances in the middle of the day, unaware of the horror they signaled. One of the things Didi was going to do, among all of the other things, was to get a fine job and get Tony and her mother out of the neighborhood. She would get them away from the junkies and the dope and the stealing and the cheap wine smells that filled the halls and dulled the crispness of the morning. That's what Didi would do. She would lead her family out of the poverty that sucked on them, night and day.

But when she came home and found Tony lying across the armchair, it all changed. Funny—at first when she saw him, she thought that he had just drifted off, like their mother. She stood and looked at him, then bent over at the waist so she could see him better.

"Tony," she called to him, "you okay?"

The television was on, a soap opera, and she sat on the hassock and half looked at it, wondering what she should do about Tony. Then something caught her eye. At first she didn't make it out too clearly under the paper. She went and lifted the paper and saw the syringe and the cap. Tony had shot up some dope.

Sick. She wanted to throw up, to vomit. She wanted to puke. She reeled around the room. There was a violent pain in her stomach, as if someone had punched her harder than she had ever been punched before. There were tears of rage spitting from her eyes as she flung her head from side to side. Rage. She stopped and looked at Tony. He was breathing easily. She resumed her anger for a moment and then felt it subside quickly, as defeat tore it from her. She sat on the faded slipcovers, exhausted.

It was Tony in the chair, and more. It was Tony, family, blood, flesh, color, curled in living death on the chair. It was the nightmare she always knew was just around the corner. Now it was rearing its ugly, leering head toward her. Jumping up in her face, grinning her down. Getting bad. She had always thought about the nightmare, thought of how the young sisters would greet it and walk with it, and how the young brothers would stand on the corners and nod to it in the sultry Harlem summers.

"What's wrong with our black chillens today," her grandmother Hattie would say, pulling at the dark dress she invariably wore that was always riding up her far too ample flesh. "In my day chillens would go to church and try to stay in the way of Jesus. Today kids ain't a bit more steadin' about Jesus than take wings and fly. All they want to do is to make babies and mess with that dope. These young gals can't keep their dresses down, and I don't know what these boys see in this dope business. It ain't nothing but a crying shame what these kids be doing."

Didi wanted to cry and wanted to hurt Tony. She wanted to go up side his head and ask him what he thought he was doing. And she didn't want an answer, either. But she knew it wouldn't do any good. He had already got into his smart-mouth ways. The first time Didi saw him hanging out with Billy "Touchy" Jenkins, she knew something bad would come of it.

Touchy came from garbage. His father was a wife beater, and his mama was one of those sneaky chicks who thought she was cute. They were made for each other and little Billy Jenkins was just what they deserved. Then he grew up and got into dope. He dressed clean and wore gold chains around his neck and didn't want anyone to touch him because he was so precious.

"I don't know why you got to hang out with that man," Didi said to Tony once; she was ironing a skirt and hoping it wouldn't get shiny. "In the first place he's twice your age, and he's not—do you think he's something special because he stands around on a street corner in silk pants looking like some kind of sissy?"

"Who I be with is my business," Tony said.

"Sure, it's your business because you don't have an answer. Touchy's into anything he can get his hands on, and you know it."

"You running that jive down because you got blinkers on," Tony said. "What it's about is staying clean and living the way you want to live. Some dude said that if you live the way you want to live, you cool. The white man stay clean and live the way he want to live, and you think that's okay because he doing his white thing and you dig it. Touchy staying clean and doing his thing and you don't dig it, that's all."

"Uh-huh, I see you didn't say he was doing a black thing."

"I ain't into that black and white crap." Tony looked into the mirror and wiped an imaginary speck from his face, which was maturing from cute to handsome. "I got to keep my mind thinking on how Tony is going to get over. You got them books you be hitting all the time, that's your thing. I got my concentration."

"Your concentration?" Didi put the iron down.

"Ain't nobody stupid, girl," Tony said. "Just some people can't keep their minds on what they doing. They go out here and party a little and hustle a little and they think they're getting over. Getting over is a thing all by itself. That's what Touchy's about."

"I figured he taught you that."

Now Didi looked at him, sprawled across the chair, high on shooting up something. There was no way she was going to talk to him, no way at all. He would just come up with something stupid that he thought was smart.

Didi got up and walked downstairs. She didn't know what she was going to say, exactly, but she knew who she was going to say it to.

"Okay, now what exactly is your complaint, miss?" The desk sergeant looked down at her.

"My brother is using drugs," Didi said carefully. "He's getting the drugs from this guy named Touchy Jenkins, and I want him arrested."

"You want your brother arrested or the other guy?"

"Arrest them both, what difference does it make?" Didi asked.

"Well, it makes a big difference," the sergeant said. "In the first place, we're not going to arrest your brother just because he's a user. If we did that, we'd have to arrest every third person on the street. Now, if you want us to arrest this other guy—"

"Touchy Jenkins."

"Okay, we have to have some hard evidence. You can't just walk up to people and start snatching them off the streets."

"All you have to do is to go up there and take a look at what they're doing and you can see them dealing," Didi said.

"Do you have any hard evidence?" the sergeant asked. "Have you ever dealt with this guy personally."

"No, I haven't," Didi said. She could feel her anger rising.

"Then what I suggest you do is to get your brother to

a clinic, one of those halfway houses **or** something like that, and concentrate on worrying about him. I'll turn in your report and—"

The sergeant watched Didi whirl around and walk away.

"What's with the cutie?" a young patrolman asked.

"Her brother's a junkie," the sergeant said. "You know, all you'd have to do is give pistols to everyone up here like that girl and declare an open season on pushers. You'd have Harlem free of dope overnight."

"She have any names?"

"One. I think the narc squad knows him, but I'll turn it in."

Everybody in the neighborhood knew that Touchy Jenkins didn't play. The thing he had learned first in life was that you didn't play with people and you didn't let people play with you. One of the earliest things Touchy remembered, from the time when he lived across from Joint Diseases Hospital, was when his aunt had come and given him five dollars. It was two days after Easter, and he was the only kid around who hadn't got anything. He didn't get any colored eggs or jelly beans or chocolate bunnies. Nothing.

"What happened to your Easter basket?" Aunt Mavis had asked him.

"He ate the whole thing up the first day," his father said. "Didn't even offer me or his mother nothing."

"Billy, why you so greedy?" Mavis had asked. "If I give you this five-dollar bill, you gonna spend it up in one day?"

"No, ma'am," he had said.

Mavis gave him the five-dollar bill, and he kept it until she went to the bathroom and his father took it.

"I'm going to buy an Easter basket with it," Touchy said, remembering the ones that were reduced for the after-Easter sale. "Can I buy it tomorrow?"

"Not if you keep running your mouth," his father said. "Now, why don't you go on out and play."

And later, when his aunt had left and he asked his father for the money back, his father asked why Touchy had let him take it in the first place.

"You ain't man enough to hang on to your money," his father had said, "you ain't supposed to have it."

If you weren't man enough to hang on to your reputation, you weren't supposed to have that, either. That's what Touchy had now, a reputation for not playing and for taking care of business when business needed to be taken care of.

When the man from downtown came uptown to do business, Touchy was just as clean as the biggest dealers in Harlem. He didn't hold nothing back, he wasn't late, and he was always straight in his dealings. He didn't let anything slide, and when there was more territory to walk into, the downtown people always knew who could handle it. They didn't want trouble, and neither did Touchy. That's why he wasn't about to let some dumb broad blow his cool. Not that she could mess with him, because he stayed correct. He didn't touch anything illegal, he didn't use nothing illegal, and he didn't handle any money. The only thing he carried with him was his driver's license for I.D. and ten crisp one-hundred-dollar bills. But when people started dropping dimes, somebody had to answer.

"Man, who is this broad?"

"Tony's sister. Nice-looking mama. Light brown, got a real fine way of talking."

"Tony, that kid that hangs around, act like he think he somebody?"

"Yeah, that's him. He using now."

"Get somebody to mess her up a little, let her know who she dealing with. I don't want nothing heavy. Can't stand nothing this close to home."

"Yeah, okay."

"What's wrong with the broad anyway?"

"She looking out for him."

"Don't he hang out with Jimmy D and Lavelle?"

"Yeah."

"Good, have them kick his sister's butt."

CHAPTER II

DIDI RAN IT DOWN ANYWAY, EVEN THOUGH SHE KNEW THAT Tony wouldn't listen.

"All you living for is to be a junkie?" She was making eggs and sausages. In the pan the sausage patties sizzled as they browned quickly. "Because if you're a junkie that's all you live for, and you know it, Tony."

"Why do I have to hear your mouth?" Tony asked. "I mean, is your mouth the price I got to pay for the sausages?

Because if it is, I best get myself down to the greasy spoon—
the price is cheaper."

"Uh-huh." Didi nodded knowingly at him. "You can
come up with some lip, but you can't come up with an
answer, can you?"

"Shut up!"

"Shut *me* up!" Didi picked up the skillet with the sausages. "If you so bad with your dope self, shut *me* up."

Tony got up and grabbed his shirt from the back of the
chair and headed out the door.

If there was anything he didn't want to hear it was Didi's
mouth. He knew what he was doing. He had been using
a little too much, but he knew that. He was aware of what
it was all about, and in the awareness was control. He was
cutting back, stepping down. It had come to him once on
a park bench, when he woke up with his watch and wallet
gone. It had been a warm day but he felt cold with the
vision of himself nodding out on the bench. He had seen
suckers nodding on the benches or under the stairs or any-
place else where they could find a shadow or create one
in their minds for the brief moments it took them to get
off. He had thought about kicking out cold, putting it all
down at once, taking the agony and doing it, just doing it,
but it hadn't worked out. He had told himself what he
was going to do, but when the time came, when the time
came, he was cooking and twisting around to find a vein
and telling himself that at least he would never free-
base.

Then the thought came to him to try just to cut it down,
a little less every time. He would measure it out and cool

it a little at a time. Maybe it still wouldn't be easy, but that was cool, too. He didn't expect it to be easy.

But he didn't want to hear Didi's mouth. All the crap she was busting over his head didn't mean a thing, because he had heard it all before. Now it was get-down time with his own jones, and the truth didn't mean a thing. What he would do was to get clean again, and then he would become a stone businessman. Square business. What he would do would be to use his touch with the life to keep himself straight.

Didi was cool. The chick dug him. His sister was the only person in the world who loved him. Sometimes, when things were going just right, his mother was cool, too. But even though he knew that she loved him sometimes, when things were just right, it wasn't the same as with Didi. Didi was a damn rock. She meant him cool. That's how he felt before he found out that Didi had dropped a dime on Touchy.

"Man, how you do that?" he had asked. "How you do that? The word all over the street is that you went down to the precinct and dropped a dime on Touchy!"

"What I'd like to do is to drop a brick on his butt," Didi said.

"Wait a minute!" Tony grabbed Didi by the arm. "Are you some kind of fool or something? Touchy don't be playing this kind of television garbage!"

"Oh, what he *be* playing, Tony?" Didi wrenched her arm loose from her brother. "Check yourself out looking for a vein to stick a needle in and tell me what Touchy *be* playing."

Tony was scared. He remembered when Eddie DeJesus had tried to rip Touchy off about a year before and they found Eddie OD'd on a roof. The papers just said that he was found dead, but the word on the block was that Touchy had got to him.

Tony didn't know what to do. He thought about staying low for a while, but he didn't think that was the way to play it. He had to bring it out in the open. When he heard that Touchy's car was parked on the block, he went to it. Big as daylight, walking slow, past the eyes checking him out. Carlos, Touchy's main boy, was leaning against the car. He saw Carlos bend over and say something into the car.

"What's happening?" Tony asked.

"You tell me." Carlos didn't look at him. A toothpick dangled from his lips.

"Got to talk to Touchy."

"Talk."

"Hey, Touchy." Tony leaned into the car window. Touchy sat in the big back seat of the Lincoln; his light blue silk suit looked good against the dark blue interior. "I just wanted to let you know that my sister—Didi, you know her?"

Touchy didn't answer.

"Well, she went and blabbed a lot of crap to the Man," Tony said. "You know what I mean?"

"Yeah," Touchy said. "But do you know what *I* mean?"

"What did you say?" Tony asked.

"I got to say something for you to know where I'm at?"

"No," Tony said. "I just wanted to let you know."

Tony walked away from the car in awkward steps, not stepping on the cracks in the sidewalk, feeling Carlos's eyes on his back. It would blow over. Things would be cool again. Things always got cool again on the streets.

"What Touchy say?" Reggie asked Lavelle.

"Said to teach her a lesson," Lavelle said. "First thing she got to know is that the Man came over himself and told Touchy about how she was running off at the mouth. Then after she knows that, she got to feel some pain."

"He want to mess her up good?" Reggie said.

"He said just bruise her a little." Jimmy D was sucking on a bottle of Coke. "The way I feel, since we got to mess her up anyway, we might as well cop some loving from her, too."

"Touchy say that all right?"

"Didn't ask him," Jimmy D said. "But he was thinking about cutting her up. Now if he thought about that, I know he ain't got no feeling for the chick."

"You say she come down this street just about four?" Reggie asked.

"Yeah. I figured we take her into the hallway, maybe even up on the roof. She give us any crap, we tell her we gonna throw her off."

"How she gonna give us any crap when we three and she ain't but one?" Reggie said. "You thinking like that, no wonder you got me in on the deal."

"Ain't nobody got you in on the deal because of her," Lavelle said. "Just that Touchy didn't tell Tony what he was going to do. I don't want to go through no hassle kicking his butt. I don't mind kicking it, though. I can't stand no pretty boys, and that's what that chump is, a pretty boy."

"I'da made Tony kick her butt," Jimmy D said. "It's his sister, man. And not only that, if he had been cool with hisself, she couldn't have peeped his action from the get go."

"This her coming now, ain't it?"

Motown saw the girl going down the street and the three dudes jumping up into her face. First he thought they were just making a play for her, but then one of them punched her in the stomach. Something inside Motown tightened up, but he didn't move. He just turned kind of sideways and checked it out. They had her arms behind her back and were trying to push her into the building across from where he was staying.

Maybe if he hadn't seen her around, minding her own business and staying by herself, he could have just walked away. Maybe if he hadn't known the dudes. He wasn't no hero. He didn't dig getting into nobody else's mess.

He walked down the block. Maybe they see him coming they just leave the girl and split. He walked down the block near the curb so they could see him coming. But they had pushed her inside the building.

Motown went into the hall and saw them near the staircase. Two of them were trying to pull the girl up the stairs. The other one was trying to get his hand under her dress.

Even as he was trying to think of what to do, Motown was swinging. He caught one of them, the one with his hand halfway under the girl's dress, on his cheekbone.

29:

There was fear. In the dark, pee-smelling hallway there was fear—three against one was time for fear. Motown swung again and hit another one of them. The third put a fat hand in Motown's face and pushed him against the wall. His head hit hard. There was a moment of confusion—was it a full second?—and another blow got him. He lifted his foot and kicked out blindly. There was a grunt. He twisted himself in the direction of the door, realizing that someone was holding him around the waist but that he wasn't really hurt. He swung again from the shoulder, turning into the punch, driving his fist between two wide eyes.

He brought his fist back again but had to bring it down as the arms around his waist lifted him off the ground. It had to be Reggie! Motown dug his heel into a knee and straightened his leg hard, letting the side of his shoe scrape against shin bone. The arms around his waist released their grip.

Motown could hear the girl's screams. For a moment, over someone's back, clutching for the face of one of the others, Motown's face came within inches of the girl's.

There were footsteps behind him. He turned to see one of them running toward the door that led to the street. Motown braced himself against the wall. Lavelle was trying to get off the floor where he had fallen in the scuffle. Maybe Motown had knocked him down. He was trying to get up and Motown kicked him in the side of his knee. He dragged himself up and half-ran, half-limped toward the street. Then it was the girl, wild-eyed, her mouth open and framing the stillborn scream within her, bolting past him from the terror of the hallway. Then it was just him and Reggie. Reggie was behind him, trying to get his arm around Motown's neck.

He grabbed the back of Reggie's head, grabbed a chunkful of thick hair, and pulled it back. Reggie released him and stepped to the side. He swung for Motown's stomach and dug his fist into the hard flesh.

Too hard. Life wasn't that easy that you could be weak. You had to be strong. You did a thousand million pushups and situps and deep knee bends in the darkness of your room each night because you couldn't be weak in this world, you couldn't be weak and let people know it. Otherwise they would come and find you, huddled in the corner under the blanket that you had had for as long as you remembered, trembling in the darkness. You did the pushups and the situps and the deep knee bends until you were so exhausted that you would fall asleep without thinking, without reliving a single moment of the life you had lived or would have to live.

Too hard. Motown was too hard for anyone. Too hard for Reggie to hurt him. There had been a time when Reggie could have hurt him, could have found him weak and alone in the world and afraid of the next day and what it would bring. But not now.

Motown hit Reggie with all of his force and felt the bones beneath the flesh quiver. He hit him again, pushing the thought of his own past weakness into Reggie's body. Reggie was breathing hard, trying to cover up. Now they were apart. Reggie was looking at him. There was bewilderment in Reggie's face. Later, after the heart had slowed and the mind had ceased its panic, there would be pain in the flesh, but for now there was only bewilderment. Reggie looked at Motown. The face looked familiar. Familiar and somehow not familiar. He backed away, and then made for the door. Whoever it was standing there, half hidden in the darkness of the hallway, owning the shadows that surrounded him, he was too hard.

Breathe again, he told himself. Walk slowly down the corridor into the coolness of the evening. Would anyone be waiting outside for him to resume the fight? Did it matter? No. He walked to the door. There was the smell of dried blood in his nostrils. The air was cool. A slight breeze touched his cheek gently. He checked the buttons on his shirt by letting a finger run down easily across his chest. He wasn't breathing hard. His pulse had slowed. He looked along the street and saw people walking along, minding whatever business they had to mind. A brother was coming out of the chicken-and-rib place with a piece of chicken in one hand and his handkerchief in the other, dabbing at his face between bites. Motown checked the street and walked across slowly to where he was staying.

Didi ran into the bathroom. She looked in the mirror and didn't recognize herself. Her hands were still shaking. God, but she felt dirty. She wanted to take a bath but didn't want to take her clothes off. She had locked the door and put the chain on, but she checked it again. Her mother wasn't home and neither was Tony. She ran the water and began bathing. She couldn't cry. She wanted to, but she couldn't. She felt dirty, almost ashamed of herself.

It was about her telling the police about Tony using drugs and about Touchy selling the stuff on the streets. That's what it was about. They had spit it into her face. Laughing at her because she had thought that the law would protect her.

Then they had dragged her into that hallway.

"You better put your hands on your mama!" she had said.

One of them grabbed her hair. She was fighting them, then her arms were behind her back and she was bent over, being pushed up the steps. She felt a hand go under her dress. She tried to twist away. Panic. She couldn't stop the panic. It was real, pushing and pulling at her clothes, punching at her. It was real and not real—a dream, a nightmare. Two of them slapping her and the other one, an animal, reaching for her private parts, grasping in the darkness for her soul. And her too much afraid to be angry.

In the bathtub she was angry. She became even more angry. She scrubbed fiercely at the parts they had reached. Her knees. Her thigh, until the flesh reddened. Her arms.

She hated as she had never hated before, hate that crawled along her skin and coursed through her bone marrow. Hate that became present thought and memory.

She would get a butcher knife and stalk the streets until she found Touchy. Then she would go up to him, she would be a wild person, flying across the sidewalk. No, she would screech herself through time and space, a wailing banshee, an ugly piercing scream that would tear into Touchy's bosom and destroy him.

They would drag her off his dying carcass, transformed by her hand into a formless lump. They would try her and put her in jail, and she would sit in her cell for years, stoically, without speaking a single word.

Then they would let her out. Her hair would be white and the flesh would droop from her arms with old age. She would read somewhere about a man who had risen from the ghetto despite the fact that his father was the notorious dope pusher Touchy Jenkins, and who had become decent and was raising a family in Riverdale. And she would go and kill him and go to jail again and hope to live until the son of the son rose so that she could kill him, too.

And it wasn't true. This she knew: It wasn't true that she could kill anyone. If he had been there at the moment she could have/would have killed him, but even now, sitting in the tub, her anger was being pushed into memory by frustration.

"The cops told Touchy that you were down at the precinct running your mouth," one of them had said. "You think that something going on on *Touchy's* streets he don't know about? That what you think, girl?"

The water had turned cold. She got out of the tub. She was sore now, and there was an ugly bruise on her hip. She looked again into the mirror. Her face was swollen. She was ugly. She went and put on some clean clothes, her jeans. She made tea. There were two roaches near the garbage bag. The tears came. They filled the room and pushed at the walls. But they didn't last the way she had thought they would, the way they had when she found out that she wouldn't get a full scholarship, that in all probability she wouldn't go to college. The tears didn't last that long this time. Perhaps she just had less of them.

Later, when Didi thought more about what had happened in the hallway, she remembered the shadow person who was suddenly there with them. The shadow person, a shadow among shadows. She remembered seeing him fighting her attackers. She remembered an instant when she stood next to him, both of them pushing away one of the guys who'd been holding her against the wall just moments before. She had run at the first opportunity, run toward the front door, leaving him to the grunts and the groans and the whacking of flesh behind her. What happened then? Had he been killed? Had he been beaten up? Who was he?

She thought back. Wait. From somewhere in her mind, from a corner, from a darkness, she remembered him. She had seen him in the street by himself. Always walking closer to the buildings than she thought an honest person should. Who was he? A nothing person? That's what she called them, nothing people. People who went from the magic of childhood into nothingness. Teenage boys standing on the corner waiting for nothing to happen, laying their traps to catch the moment, punctuating it by abusing themselves or some sister.

Who had she seen him speaking to? Tutmose—down at the corner selling newspapers. She had seen him speaking to Tutmose. She thought of going to find him, to say something to him perhaps. Not thank you, because she didn't know his motivation. She didn't know what beast lurked in his chest, what had brought him into the hall. She had to say something to him. But not tonight. Tonight she would sit quietly and mourn for herself. In the morning, if she still lived, there would still be time to find the boy.

There wasn't much sleep that night. A start here and there, a snatch of blackness interrupted by violence, jerking her into the reality of a fearful present, triggered by some noise, some creaking, some rattling in the alleyway between her building and the next. At the sound of a car horn, Didi said to herself, "God, I am made for better things than this. I am made for better things than this." She had said this many times to herself before, but this time she wasn't sure.

Tony skulked into the house. He had heard what had happened.

Yeah, yeah—maybe it was all cool, he thought to himself. Maybe Didi learned her lesson to keep her nose out of other people's business.

He moved quietly in the dark, undressing, not wanting to see her, not wanting her to see him. He had his fixings with him. He took a chance and cooked it in his room, hoping that Didi wouldn't smell it. He cooked it, watching the white powder liquefy in the greenish light from a neon sign across the street. He watched it suck up into the syringe, and then he put it in his vein. He put the syringe away and stretched out on his bed. The rush wasn't that much. He knew it wouldn't be, but he didn't feel sick anymore. He didn't feel good, but for the moment at least there was an absence of pain. He watched the dim green light on the ceiling flicker on and off and then slowly drifted away.

In the morning Didi put on jeans and a tank top and sneakers. If they were going to attack her again she would be ready this time. She tried to muster up some anger and she couldn't, but she wasn't afraid, either. No, she wasn't afraid. She thought of going downtown to a movie just to get away from the neighborhood. She came out of the room. There was Tony standing in front of the stove. He was frying eggs. She had thought about making tea, but when she saw her brother she changed her mind.

"Heard you had some trouble yesterday." Tony glanced at her and then quickly looked away.

"Don't speak to me. Don't speak to me. Just don't speak to me."

"Hey, don't blame me for your troubles, mama."

"Don't speak to me, Tony. Do *not* speak to me!"

Tony stammered out a word and then watched it fall leadenly between the two of them. He turned the light off under the eggs, looked at them, and then walked past Didi to his room.

Didi went to the stove, finished cooking the eggs, put them on a plate and ate them herself. Tony knew he was wrong. Tony was not a dumb kid—he knew he was wrong. She began to cry again and was annoyed at herself for crying, for weakness, for tears, for the way her hands trembled. She didn't respect weakness. You didn't get out of traps by being weak. And that's what she was in, a trap. A trap of dope and noncaring people, perhaps not even real people.

She finished the eggs, went in to see if her mother was still asleep, saw that she was, and left without saying good-bye. She went downstairs. She went to the corner where Tutmose was selling newspapers and asked him about the boy who had helped her.

"I think he lives in buildings, in old buildings or something. He's dark. Real, real dark. He's got high shoulders. I've seen you talking to him," she said.

"Tutmose talk to a lot of people. Who you mean? Who you mean?" Tutmose repeated himself.

"I don't know his name. He doesn't hang out very much. He's always by himself."

"You mean Motown. That's who you mean. You talking about Motown. Everybody talking about Motown. He had a fight with some of Touchy's people. They say he messed them suckers up."

"Do you know where he is now?"

"Yeah, but, you know Tutmose—I mean, I'm his friend. I don't know. What you want him for?"

"None of your business what I want him for. Do you know where he is now or do you not know where he is now?" Didi asked, stepping in front of Tutmose so that he could see she meant business.

"Yeah, he down there. You know that he's in 317."

"You're sure?"

"Yeah, I'm sure. Why I say that if I ain't sure?"

Didi turned and went down the street. She knew which building 317 was. It used to be a nice building. It used to be a building full of young black families. Some of her friends had lived in that building at one time. There had been talk about the building being renovated, but instead of being renovated, it had simply been abandoned like so much of Harlem, the buildings and the lives. She walked boldly to 317, not because she felt so bold but to cover up the fear that was in her stomach. What had happened in the hallway was still with her. She was waiting for them to come and bother her again. She didn't know what they were going to do, but she knew that what had happened had settled in her stomach and cramped her bowels and made her feel weak.

The stairway in 317 was still in fairly good shape. There were newspapers strewn over it and here and there an old cigarette butt. The hallways smelled of urine and worse. She went up to the second floor listening for sounds, making as much noise as she could so that if the boy was there, he would hear her coming. And he did.

"What you want here?" He was standing in the hallway near an open door, one hand in front of him with his thumb hooked into his belt, the other behind him.

"You're the guy that came into the hallway yesterday, aren't you?" Didi asked.

"Yeah," Motown answered.

"I came to say thank you, " Didi said, standing at the top of the stairs.

"Oh," Motown said. A moment of silence. "That's okay."

"You—live here?" Didi asked, feeling that the thank you that she had offered somehow was not quite enough.

"Sometimes," Motown said.

"In there?"

"Yeah." Motown relaxed his body and Didi saw that he had a small baseball bat in his other hand.

"Why?"

"Why I live here?"

"No," Didi said. "Why did you come into the hallway?"

"I don't know."

Didi walked over to where Motown stood and looked past him into the apartment. It was furnished, probably with odds and ends that he had found throughout the building. The floor was clean. There was a picture of a black knight on the wall.

"May I see your place?" Didi asked. Motown shrugged and walked into his home.

"It ain't much," he said. "I'm, you know, thinking about fixing it up, maybe even moving. Getting a regular place."

Didi walked in behind him. It looked terrible once she had walked in. She had never imagined a person as young as this boy would ever live in a place like this.

"My name is Didi. Didi Johnson," she said.

"I'm—my name is Frank but everybody call me Motown."

"Oh, who's everybody?"

"Everybody," Motown answered. "I don't talk to a lot of people."

"I know," Didi said. "I've seen you around."

"I've seen you around, too," Motown said.

"I really appreciate you coming in and helping me yesterday. I hope there's no more trouble. It was a very brave thing for you to do."

"I didn't mind," Motown said.

"Why *do* you live here?"

"Good a place as any," he answered.

"You run away from home or something?" Didi asked.

"Kind of," Motown answered. "My folks got killed on a ferry. There was a fire. They never did find my father. Mostly I used to live with foster people."

"What's that?" Didi asked. "Those places where they pay people to care for you?"

"Uh-huh."

"So why you living here now?"

"I couldn't stand no more foster homes," Motown said.

"Do you—do you like it here?"

"Nothing wrong with it," Motown said defensively. "A lot of people live worse off than this."

"I didn't mean anything by it," she said.

"Then why you say it?"

"No reason. No reason at all," Didi said. "Anyway, I came to say thank you."

"Yeah. Okay." Motown looked away.

"Do you—do you need anything?"

"What you mean?"

"I've got five dollars."

"Don't need your five dollars. Man, get on out of here with your five dollars."

"Yeah. Okay. Fine. Thank you and good-bye," Didi said.

"Yeah."

She turned and walked quickly out of the room into the dark hallway. She felt her way along the banister, then stopped for a moment. She heard the scurrying of mice and then went slowly down the stairs. Suddenly there was a light on the stairs and she looked up. He was standing there with a flashlight.

"There's some tin on the stairs," he said. "Watch yourself."

"Okay," Didi said. There was a moment of silence. "Thanks."

Motown went back into his room and thought about the girl. He hadn't thought much about the fight in the hallway. He had had fights before. The guys were messing over her, and he gave her a hand. Didi. It was nice of her to come to his place, but it made him feel bad. He didn't want her to see him like this. Not that she meant anything to him, but he wished he had a swell place. Then she would have walked in and she would have said, "Hey, he lives all by himself but he got a nice place." And then maybe she would have walked away and thought about him all day long. She come up and see him like this and she was going to think that he wasn't nothing but a bum. She come offering him five dollars. Why she do that? She didn't have to do that. He wasn't a bum. Maybe he wouldn't even wait until he had more money to get a regular place. Maybe he would just go out and get it anyway.

He looked around the room. The books that the Professor had given him on African history were in the corner. He wished they had been out so she could have seen them. He had seen her going to school, carrying her books. If she had seen the books that the Professor had given him— oh, well, she was gone now. She was probably thinking she was sorry she even came up. Sorry that it had been him that had come into the hall and helped her out. Probably a lot of guys would have helped her out 'cause she was fine. She was as fine as she wanted to be.

Motown studied the room, trying to put himself in Didi's place, to see what she had seen. He didn't like any of it. It had been the first time that a girl had come to where he was staying. He should have thought about it. He should have thought that maybe she would come and say something like what she did. If he'd thought about it, he would have fixed up the place a little. There wasn't too much he could have done, but he could have put the books where she would have seen them.

Didi was walking down the street when she saw a couple of dudes standing across from her in front of the barber shop, talking to Carlos. She crossed over, walked over to the barber shop, and walked in. There was Touchy in the chair. Carlos had come in behind her and stood close enough to her to grab her if she tried anything. Touchy was getting his hair cut. The barber was just finishing, patting Touchy's hair into place here and there.

"Look." Didi spoke through clenched teeth. "Why don't you just have your boy here beat me up again?"

"What you talking about, woman?" Touchy looked at Carlos.

"You know what I'm talking about. You're the one that had those guys mess with me in the hallway."

"I don't know what you're talking about. You know, people messing with you must mean you're messing with people," Touchy said.

"Well, you better have them beat me up every time they see me, because if I see Tony with anything, I mean if I just see Tony with anything that he got from you, I'm causing trouble, and I'm going to cause it in any way I can. Do you understand that? Can you understand that?"

"You better get on out of here, girl, 'fore you get hurt." Touchy said. Carlos put his arm in front of Didi and leaned over into her face.

"You better do what the man says," Carlos said.

"I heard you had your young hero come and save you from your troubles," Touchy said. "You know, your young hero ain't gonna be around all the time. So whatever trouble you were in, I would think about trying to avoid what got me into trouble if I were you. Get my meaning?"

"You better get *my* meaning," Didi said.

Carlos pushed her toward the door, roughly. She looked up at him. Tall and hatchet-faced, he wore an earring in his left ear. He smiled at her, a sinister smile. It was a smile that said that he knew what he was about and that what he was about was more powerful than anything that Didi had. She walked out of the barber shop. She felt sick walking down the street because Carlos was right. When he grinned at her as if she was some plaything, he was right. Next to what he was and without the police, she wasn't anything but a toy, something to play with, then throw away.

CHAPTER

THE WORD ON THE STREET WAS THAT THE THING BETWEEN
Tony and Touchy was over and that the two were tight
again. That's what Tutmose was telling Motown when
Didi passed by them on the corner. Motown smiled at Didi,
but she didn't smile back. Instead she just walked on by,
half wrapped in her own thoughts, half street-wary, as she
had been since the incident in the hallway.

"It was one of them things," Tutmose was saying. "You
know, like they was out but now they back again. Touchy
even turned Tony on to some methadone so he could cool
out on his habit and everything."

"Yeah."

"You find you a place yet?" Tutmose folded a paper
and whacked it against his leg as a potential customer went
by.

"I ain't looking anymore," Motown said. "I thought for
a while I was going to look around and find another place,
but now I ain't in a hurry."

"Places is hard to find," Tutmose said. "But you know
what I was thinking? I was thinking that maybe you and
me could find a place somewhere together and split the
rent."

"We'll see," Motown said.

"Okay," Tutmose said. "You want a paper?"

"Maybe later," Motown said, starting to walk away. "If you don't sell them all."

Motown liked Tutmose. He had known him for years and knew he had a good heart. Tutmose was like Motown in a lot of ways. He liked doing things that he saw people doing on television. He remembered once seeing Tutmose smoking a pipe and had asked him why he was smoking it. Tutmose told him that he had seen a guy on television smoking and the guy had looked "so cool." In the world of television, nobody was hungry and everybody had a home to go to. To Motown, it seemed right that everybody should have a home and not be hungry.

But Tutmose was slow. He was big, and he was strong, but he was slow, too. Sometimes, when Motown would want to talk to him about something serious, he couldn't understand what Motown was talking about. Then he would just smile and say that he agreed with Motown. Motown didn't know a lot about things you read in books, except about black history, but he wasn't slow. He could read well, and he could figure okay. And the important things, the things that really mattered, he could ask the Professor about.

"Time wasn't meant to drag the way it does," Oliver Harris, known as "the Professor," said. "Time was meant to fly by like the wings of a hummingbird. You know the wings of a hummingbird move so quickly you don't see any real movement at all. All you see is a blur where the wings are supposed to be. That's what life is supposed to be all about. You should be living your life so fully, so beautifully, that time is just a blur of days and weeks and months. What you think makes the days slow down, Motown?"

"I don't know," Motown said.

"Evil slows them down," the Professor said. "Evil drags on time and makes it a painful thing. You ever notice how time flies by when you're enjoying yourself? That's because you don't have any evil in your heart to slow you down."

"I know what you mean," Motown said. Motown sipped the herbal tea that the Professor had prepared.

"So what you been doing with your life, youngblood?" the Professor asked. "You been doing yourself any good?"

"I don't know," Motown said. "I read that book you gave me on Marcus Garvey. I wished I could have met him."

"Young as you are, you probably would have been disappointed in him if you had met him." The Professor held his cup under his nose and smelled the tea. "Young people want their heroes bigger than life instead of being full of life. I hope you ain't getting into any more fights."

"No," Motown said, grinning. The sun was across the bottom of his face. "Things have cooled out pretty good on the block. Touchy and Tony, they tight again."

"Now run that thing by me one more time, boy." The Professor leaned forward. "That Touchy is a dope dealer, isn't he?"

"Yeah," Motown said. "And Tony's sister went to the cops on account of Tony was using dope. Then Touchy got mad and had some guys try to mess up Tony's sister."

"And the way I remember it," the Professor said, "he was mad at Tony, too."

47:

"Yeah."

"And what happened to make him not mad?" the Professor asked.

"I don't know," Motown said.

"Why don't you think about it?" the Professor said. " 'Cause it don't make a whole lot of sense to me. Maybe you can figure it out. Why should a man be so mad at a man so much that one day he's ready to have his sister beat up and the next day he ain't even mad?"

Motown thought that it was more than one day, but he knew that the Professor must have known it was more than one day, too. But now since the Professor had said it, had put it on the table between them, it did sound funny.

Motown bothered Didi. He didn't seem like anything much. He seemed to be what she wanted to get away from. She didn't want to be in Harlem, in anybody's ghetto, or around anyone who lived like Motown lived. What kind of a name was that anyway? Motown was a record company, and he probably thought it was cool because the record company had a big name.

But Motown bothered her. He hadn't said anything when he came into the hall. He had just come in and done what he had to do, or rather, what he didn't have to do. And when she went to his place to thank him, he didn't have much to say. He wasn't friendly. But when she had needed a light to go down the stairs, he had one and lit her way. He had smiled at her when she passed him and the guy selling newspapers that day. It was a shy smile, the kind of a smile boys had when they didn't know what to say to a girl. She had thought about smiling back, but then she was past him, the moment gone. He was good-looking in a rough kind of way, too. He had those big eyes that would have looked better if he didn't always look down. His smile was okay, too. Not even a smile, really, more like a grin. Crooked. That's what it was. Crooked. One side of his mouth would curl up and his teeth would show. He probably didn't smile because his teeth were so white. His neck was too thick, though. It made him look shorter than he was, which was probably almost six feet. He would have looked more graceful if his neck were thinner, she thought.

Motown was the kind of guy she wanted to stay away from. She had seen a hundred, no, a thousand of them, with hard flat bellies and shoulders that tilted skyward when they laughed. She had seen hundreds of them, no, thousands of them—tall, and hard and black in their springtime years and slowly drifting, drooping, bowed down and beaten down as they reached what should have been the fullness of their manhood. Didi wanted more than that. She wanted something that she could put together with her own strength and determination, something she wouldn't have to leave to the failing of any man. Still, Motown bothered her.

"Hey, man, what it's all about is dealing when the dealing has to get done." Touchy picked an imaginary speck off of his suit. "What you did was cool because you held your act together when your sister was about ready to blow everything away."

"Hey, man, she's a strange chick," Tony said. "What

she's into mostly is the Joan of Arc bag. She thinks she's going to save the world when the world don't need her saving it."

"Yeah, I'm hip," Touchy said. "Look, I got to ask you for a favor, and like I said, I think you're hip enough to take care of business for me."

"What is it?" Tony was feeling sick. He hadn't had anything since he woke up at seven-thirty, and it was almost one now. He had told Touchy that he was getting straight. He had even thanked him for supplying him with methadone to stretch out his habit so he could manage it. Touchy asked him if he was straight, and he had said just about. But just about meant going downtown to get what he didn't get from Touchy to keep himself together.

"The people downtown want me to handle more business," Touchy said. "I thought I'd put some stuff on the street around a Hundred and Fiftieth. Carlos is going to run it for me, and I thought you could go along with him just to check out the reaction. We ain't even going to charge for it at first, just let everybody cop for air so they can check out our product. What you say?"

"I can't make it," Carlos said, before Tony could answer. "I got to get downtown because my old lady is sick. She might have to have an operation. They supposed to know this afternoon."

"She still sick?" Touchy looked at Carlos. "I thought she was better?"

"I did, too," Carlos said, "until she passed out the other night. The way she went out, I thought she was dead on the spot."

"You need anything?" Touchy asked, touching his pocket where he kept his wallet.

"No, I'm okay," Carlos said. "But I wouldn't feel right if she died and I didn't even go to the hospital."

"Yeah, that's cool," Touchy said. "I can dig it. You got wheels?"

"Yeah."

"You go on down to the hospital, and if you need anything, you just give me a call."

Carlos left and Touchy dialed a number. He asked whoever it was that answered the phone for someone named Webster, listened a moment, and then hung up in disgust.

"Things ain't going my way," Touchy said. "Ain't nobody available to take care of business. My man Webster got busted for some jive charge and got ten days in jail in Jersey City. Now ain't that a trip? The man's doing a half-million dollars a year in drugs and gets a ten-day rap for emptying an ashtray out his car window. Ain't that a trip?"

"Yeah." Tony was getting to feel really bad. He hoped that Touchy wasn't going to stick him with a long conversation. He had to go out and cop something quick or he'd be in trouble.

"Look, man, what you doing?"

"Nothing much," Tony said.

"You drive?"

"I don't have a license," Tony said.

"I didn't ask you if you had a license," Touchy said. "I asked you if you drove."

"Yeah."

"Then why don't you go on and pick this stuff up instead

of Carlos and take it and pass it around. I got about five thousand dollars' worth of stuff to put on the street. Ain't nothing to it. Just go around where the junkies be at and pass it around. We do that a couple of times, and then we go up and start hustling the stuff. The more that's on the street, the more they going to need and they'll get the bread. You handle that?"

"Yeah," Tony said.

"Take this number down," Touchy said, pushing the phone toward Tony. "Go over to a Hundred Fortieth. It's building 244. Go up to the top-floor landing. There should be a bag of garbage on the stairs leading up to the roof. Dump the bag and on the bottom you should find the stuff. If you get up there and it ain't there, call me and let me know. You got that?"

"Yeah."

"Now if it ain't there you got to call me right away," Touchy said. "Because I done already put out the money."

Tony licked his lips when Touchy wasn't looking and tried to ignore the nausea he was feeling. Once he got into the open air he knew it wouldn't be so bad. He wrote down the telephone number and stooped to untie and tie his shoelace, trying to be casual to show Touchy that he was straight. Touchy pushed the keys to his car over the desk.

"You do this little thing right," Touchy said, "and maybe you and me can do some real business. I ain't promising nothing, mind you, just a maybe."

"Hey, that's cool," Tony said, taking the keys that Touchy had pushed across the desk.

"Why don't you go on, now." Touchy had taken some

cologne out of his desk and splashed some on his face. "Soon's you get back bring me the keys."

Tony was gone less than a minute before there was a knock on Touchy's door.

"Yo, Touchy." Reggie looked into Touchy's office. "You know Tony getting into your hog?"

"Yeah," Touchy said. "He checking the drop for me. How come you checking on him—you couldn't do nothing if I told you to stop him. Three of you couldn't handle a girl. Now get on out of here."

"Yeah."

Reggie had hung around Touchy for three years and hadn't had a shot of getting into anything. One day Touchy was supposed to be mad at Tony and the next day he was letting him use his wheels. He didn't like it at all. He went on down the street. Later for Touchy.

Meanwhile, Touchy had finally gotten the number he was calling. He waited until the person who answered the phone found who Touchy was looking for.

"Hello, Carlos? Yeah, the sucker is on his way. You got in touch with the people? Okay, tell them don't be messing with my car. I don't want it towed no place, either. Them tow trucks mess up your alignment."

Touchy hung up the phone.

"The thing we all have to remember," the Professor said, "is that we're all in the tribe from the moment that we're named until the moment that the last memory of our deeds is gone. Every time we say such and such a person is no longer a member of the tribe, we weaken ourselves, because we're just as strong as the tribe. The tribe has got to have numbers and the strength of each person. You understand what I'm saying?"

"Yeah," Motown said. "I think I do."

"When you walk down the street and you see members of the tribe falling by the wayside, you have to understand that that's part of you falling over there."

"Sometimes it's hard," Motown said.

"Who you telling?" The Professor grinned. His teeth were crooked and yellow, and his wide smile seemed out of place in the full beard. "It's a poor preacher who can't preach a better sermon than he can practice. The things I tell you, boy, are things I've either lived through or some idea I've conjured up, sitting here with all these books. But when you go out in the street and you see the misery, and the wrongdoing, and the people destroying their own tribe, well, it's hard to stick with what you know is right. Your heart don't always want to follow your head. Just because a thing is right, it doesn't mean that it's easy."

"I know that," Motown said.

"What you know?" The Professor grinned at him again. "You don't even know what you know yourself. When you get out in the world and start doing, then you see what you know. Now you get that book over there and get on out of here."

"What's it about?" Motown asked.

"Just some foolishness some black man wrote about some musketeers," the Professor said. "You might as well get some foolishness in you, too."

Motown looked at the finely bound book and opened it. He flipped through the pages until he came across an illustration of a man on a horse. It did look interesting.

"I'll bring it back in a few days," Motown said.

"Motown?"

"Sir?" Motown stopped at the door.

"How you taking care of yourself, son?" The Professor's voice was soft.

"Just fine," Motown said. "I finished the book you gave me on Pushkin and I understood most of it—"

"No, no," the Professor said, standing. "I know you taking care of your mind. I can feel the hunger in you for knowledge. But are you eating okay? I worry about you at night, especially when it rains, or I hear about someone setting fires to buildings and things."

"I'm taking care of myself," Motown said. He took the Professor's hand. "I really am."

"You know if you need anything . . ."

Motown nodded and tucked the book under his arm.

It always saddened the professor to see Motown leave his bookshop. He always felt as if he was failing the boy somehow. He wanted to give him something, something more than just the hours of conversation, even more than the books. The boy had a good mind, that was true, but he needed more than that. He needed a real home and a reason to start trusting people again. Maybe, the Professor thought, there would come a time when he could reach Motown without being afraid that he would chase him away. Maybe.

Motown felt good walking across 125th Street. The Professor always made him feel good somehow. Not just good in general, either; he felt good about himself when he was with the Professor.

He stopped in at Mamie's Burgers 'N Dogs to buy a hot dog, something he knew the Professor wouldn't approve of. The Professor, who didn't eat meat of any kind, always spoke out especially about hot dogs. Said they were food to kill the soul.

"Hey, man, we got a score to settle." Reggie stood in the doorway of Mamie's and pointed his finger at Motown. There was a thin light-skinned girl with him.

"You sneaked me in the hallway, but we gonna settle our thing one of these days."

"I'm here," Motown said. "You want me, you come on over here and get me."

"I ain't having no fights in my place." Mamie waved a big butcher knife in the air. "Y'all want to fight, go on out of here."

"I got my woman with me now," Reggie said. "But I'll deal with your butt when the time is right. You can put them coins in the bank and draw interest on 'em!"

"I ain't worried about you," Motown said.

"Uh-huh. And just because that chickie's brother is driving around a Hundred and Fortieth Street in Touchy's car don't mean that I forgot about her butt, either. When the time comes, I'm dealing and I'm dealing hard!"

"I told y'all to get on out of here with that mess," Mamie said. "I got payin' customers in here."

Motown watched as Reggie and the girl with him left. He felt the heaviness in the pit of his stomach. There was no way that he was afraid of Reggie in a fair fight, but who said Reggie would come after him in a fair fight? He finished his frank slowly and left. What had Reggie said, that Tony was driving around in Touchy's car on 140th Street?

There were things going on in Motown's mind, things he didn't particularly want to sort out, or deal with directly. Part of it had something to do with what the Professor had said about everybody being a member of the tribe. Another part had to do with Tony being Didi's brother. The girl wouldn't leave his head. Her face would come to him in the middle of the night, or he would hear her voice when he knew he was alone in his place. What had she asked him? Why had he come into the hallway? He imagined her asking him that again and again. The things he would say to her kept changing, but were never quite right. He didn't know how to talk to her. The words just wouldn't come.

There were a few drops of rain falling when he reached 140th Street. He looked around until he spotted Touchy's flashy Cadillac. It was parked in front of one of the buildings, but that didn't mean that Tony was in that building. Motown thought about waiting for him on the street, maybe near the car.

There was a police car on the corner. Two police officers, one white and the other Spanish, sat in it, drinking coffee. Motown looked down the block. Something was wrong, out of place. Then he saw it. There were four little kids sitting on the stoop of a brownstone. There were three girls and a boy and they had a jumprope, but they weren't playing. They had either seen or sensed something too.

57:

Motown leaned against a building and half-closed his eyes. A tall white man, well built and wearing the gray uniform that the electric company workers used, walked slowly down the street. He stopped in front of one of the buildings and looked into the doorway. He stepped in for a moment and then came out and continued walking down the block. A dark heavy sister wearing a light tan sweater crossed bow-leggedly across the street. In her hand she clutched a book, which Motown figured to be a Bible. She stopped, once she had gained the sidewalk, to catch her breath. Then she held out her hand, palm up, to feel the rain.

Motown saw the man in the electric company uniform turn toward the police car and shrug.

A wino half-walked, half-staggered down the street. He stopped across from the police car.

"Hey!" he called out, from a distance of about twelve feet from the car. "Somebody stole my wine. I had a pint of wine and some lowdown dog done stole it!"

"What's that in your pocket?" The Puerto Rican policeman pointed toward the wino's coat pocket where the top of a bottle could be seen.

The wino looked at the policeman, then bent over to get a good look at his pocket. He saw the bottle sticking out and pointed to it, looking as if he might fall over at any minute. He reached for the pocket, missed it on the first try, then went for it again. This time he got the bottle out and held it up. There was still a quarter of a bottle left.

"They got most of it," he said. He unscrewed the top

and turned the bottle up to his already puffed lips. A member of the tribe.

Motown watched the man with the gray uniform walk back down the block. He watched to see if he would look into the same building again. He did.

Motown went to where the kids were still sitting. He wanted to look around to see if the cops were watching him, but was afraid to.

"How come you ain't jumping rope?" Motown asked.

"We don't have to jump no rope if we don't want to," a sassy little girl with beads in her cornrows said.

"How you get in that building over there with the white stoop if you don't want to go in the front door?" Motown asked.

"None of your B.I. business!" Sassy said.

"That's 'cause you don't know how to do it," Motown said.

"I can go right into that red building next to it and go through the basement," was her quick answer.

"One time when Bubba lef' his key home, he went into that other building like she talking about and went upstairs to the roof," the little boy said. "Then he come down to his place."

"Right, and his mama whipped his butt good," Sassy said. " 'Cause he wasn't supposed to be on no roof and he knew it, too."

Motown took a quarter out of his pocket and held it down at his side. He watched Sassy check out what he had in his hand before he closed it.

"Y'all don't look that smart to me," Motown said. "I

bet you can't guess what I have in my hand."

"A rock?" the boy asked.

"Nope."

"A bottle top," said a round-faced girl with an upturned nose and neatly trimmed afro.

"Nope."

"If I guess what it is, can I keep it?" Sassy looked down the street as if she wasn't really interested.

"Yeah," Motown said, "but you can't guess."

"I guess it's a quarter," Sassy said.

"How you know that?" Motown put a tough look on his face as he held his hand out with the quarter in it.

"I just knows things, honey," Sassy said, taking the quarter. "It's my nature."

Motown didn't want to venture the basement so he went to the next building. He went up the stairs, looking up the stairwell to see if there was anyone there. When he reached the top floor, he took a deep breath and stopped. He didn't know what he was going to find, if anything, or why he was sneaking around in this strange building. If Tony was fooling around with dope, it was Tony's business, he thought.

Motown went up on the roof. It was raining lightly now. He looked over to the next roof. At first he didn't see Tony. He was just crossing the low divider that separated the two roofs when he did see him, half-sitting, half-sprawled against the base of the water tower. He went over to him quickly. By the time he reached him, he saw the syringe next to him and a clear plastic envelope in his lap. Inside the envelope was a white powder that Motown figured to be some kind of dope. There was a small canvas bag next to him. It was full of the same kind of envelopes.

"Yo, man, what you doing here?" Tony opened his eyes, sensing Motown's presence.

Motown took the syringe, a piece of rubber tubing, and a tablespoon that he had found and put them in the canvas bag. He looked into Tony's face. The younger boy's eyes were glassy and the pupils of his eyes were large despite the brightness of the day.

"What are you doing here?" Motown asked.

"Everything's cool, man," Tony said, reaching for the things that Motown had gathered. "Put my stuff down."

Motown stood and tried to help Tony up. Tony swung a punch at Motown, just grazing him on the side of the head. Motown pushed him down hard, then took the stuff and went back to the roof of the building he had entered. He started down the stairs. It was an old building but it had incinerators and a place on each floor in the hallway to dump garbage. Motown dumped the dope and Tony's other stuff down the incinerator. Then he went downstairs.

Tony knew he had to get his head together, that some heavy action was going down. He pulled himself into a sitting position and looked around him. He turned around to see behind him. He was right, the stuff was gone. The same sucker that had helped Didi when Touchy's boys were teaching her a lesson had just ripped off Touchy's stuff. He looked around for him. Where did he go? He tried to stand but he was still so high he felt light-headed. He was just going to use just enough of Touchy's stuff to get his head together, so he didn't use much. It was a good thing, too, because the stuff must have been almost pure. If he hadn't taken it light, he could have overdosed.

He couldn't figure out how long it had been since the guy had ripped off his stuff, but he figured it couldn't have been that long.

He found the stairs and started down, his hands hardly feeling the banister as he went down. He was still nice. For a while there he had just about panicked when the dope he put into his veins hit him, but now it had eased off and he was just mildly high. He would get down into the street and the air would cool him out. He felt wet, like maybe he had been sweating. He remembered tussling with the dude who ripped him off. Motown. That was the sucker's name. Jive name for a jive dude. Motown.

He hit the front hall and saw the front stoop. He straightened himself up. Had to look cool, take care of business. If he didn't see Motown right away he would cruise around in Touchy's car until he saw him. He might even have to waste the dude. He was sorry about that, but business was business.

He stood on the stoop and looked around to see if he saw Motown on the street. The thought came to him that maybe Motown was still in the hallway, that he had missed seeing him. Maybe the sucker was getting high on Touchy's stuff. A white dude, one of those electric company guys who read the meters, came up on the stoop.

"Hey, man, you see a dark guy come down out of this building?" Tony asked.

"You're under arrest!" The white guy twisted Tony's arm behind his back.

"Hey, what you doing?"

Another detective came out of the basement, and the two cops in the squad car crossed the street. In a moment Tony, both arms twisted behind him, was back in the hallway.

In the darkened hallway two sets of hands went over his body. Hands probed inside his shirt, in his crotch, in his pants legs.

"Take his pants down!"

"Man, what you doing?" Tony tried to twist around to see his captors.

A rough hand pushed Tony's head down and he felt the end of a nightstick in his side.

"Where is it?" A hand grabbed Tony's throat. "Tell me where it is or I'll put a bullet in your head right here."

"I ain't got nothing, man." Tony's protest was shut off as the hand tightened around his neck.

"He's clean!"

"He's high, too, so he must have been using something. But he don't have his works on him!" A twangy voice said, "I'll check out the roof."

"Let's kill him," a young voice said. "I got a gun I picked up off a pimp over on Park Avenue.

"Yeah, okay. Push him under the stairs!"

Tony was shaking badly now. His arms were numb from being twisted behind his back and his shoulders ached. The two detectives took him to the staircase, pushed him down to the floor, and then pushed him with their feet under the staircase.

"You got the gun?"

"Yeah, I'll do it."

"No, give him one more chance to tell where he put the stuff."

"Hey, punk, you going to tell where you put the stuff or you gonna die under there?"

"I don't have anything, man, honest I don't." Tony was crying. He had gotten one hand from behind his back and was holding it in front of him, as if his outstretched fingers could possibly stop a bullet.

There were footsteps on the stairs.

"Nothing! We've been had!"

The voices went on for a while, talking about the clean bust they were supposed to have and whose rear end was going to be in a sling. Then they faded away.

Tony lay shaking and frightened in the darkness under the stairs for a long time before he realized that he was alone in the hallway. Slowly he pulled himself from beneath the stairs. He got to his feet. His shoulders were aching from having been twisted as his arms were forced behind his back. On the floor were his matches and the keys to Touchy's Cadillac. He took a deep breath and picked them up.

He went outside and looked around. The street was back to normal. Kids jumped rope across the street. Two women stood talking, shopping bags beneath their legs. A young pregnant woman sat drinking a Coke on a stoop. In front of the house, Carlos was just getting into Touchy's car.

"Hey, Carlos!" Anthony squared his shoulders as he neared the car. "Man, I almost got busted!"

"Yeah," Carlos said, his hand still on the open door of

the Cadillac. "I just saw the cops pulling away. I thought
they had you."

"No, that punk Motown ripped the stuff off when—
hey, what you doing up here?"

"Who? Me?"

CHAPTER IV

THE DOCTOR CALLED IT A STROKE. DIDI HAD BEEN STAND-
ing at the sink, peeling potatoes and talking to her mother
about El Salvador, when it happened.

"I don't know how they even know about those places,"
Darlene Johnson was saying. "I mean, one day you never
even hear about a place, and the next, that's all you hear
about."

"The thing is," Didi was saying, "that people are down
there doing things because they see a way to make some
kind of profit or something, or maybe they think the Com-
munists are going to take the place over. Something like
that. Then they start telling you about what's happening
but you don't know *why* it's happening. You know what
I mean?"

Her mother didn't answer. Didi thought that maybe she
had just lost interest in the conversation, had drifted away
into her own world the way she did so many times. She
turned and saw her mother, head down on the table, as if
she were asleep. But there was something in the way her

arm lay across the red-and-white checked tablecloth that didn't seem right. Perhaps it was the way her palm was turned slightly upward, or the fact that Darlene Johnson, who kept an immaculate house, had knocked over the salt shaker.

"Mama?"

The ambulance driver said that it looked like a heart problem, but he didn't think it was too serious because her heart was beating fairly regularly. Didi was getting into the ambulance when Tony showed up at the house. He looked a mess.

"It's Mama," was all Didi said.

Didi accompanied her mother to the hospital, watched as they wheeled her into the emergency room, and then waited outside in the busy waiting area. A nurse with heavy breasts who looked much too young for her white hair came and told Didi that they had taken her mother up to the fourth floor.

"She's awake now," she said. "The doctors are giving her a few more tests, and then you might be able to see her."

"How is she?" Didi asked.

"She looks okay," the nurse said. "But with strokes you can't tell for a while. What I think you should do is just to go on upstairs to the fourth floor and wait up there. You a religious girl?"

"Yes, ma'am."

"That's good, I'm glad to hear that. Why don't you ask the Lord to look in on your mother. I think that would be a nice thing to do."

Didi went upstairs and waited for more word on her mother. She thought of praying, as the nurse had suggested, but wondered if God would even listen to her now. She hadn't been to church for nearly three years and hadn't thought much of going, either.

Tony got to the fourth floor a half hour after Didi. "What happened?" he asked.

"Mama had a stroke."

"What's that mean?"

"You don't know what a stroke is?"

"I mean, is she going to be all right?"

"I think so. They say you can't tell right away with a stroke. You have to wait and see how much damage has been done. Where were you? How you get all messed up like that?"

"That's my business," Tony said.

"Your business, my damn foot!" Didi said, her voice rising. "When everybody's worried about you, it's everybody's business."

"I think Touchy tried to mess over me," Tony said, subdued.

"What you mean?"

"He tried to get me arrested. He asked me to pick up a package for him. I went up to do it and that guy that helped you in the hallway that time, that Motown, he came up there and took the stuff away from me."

"What stuff?"

"I don't know what was in the package," Tony said.

"I bet you don't. How he get up there?"

"I don't know," Tony said. "But when I come down

from the hallway the cops was waiting for me. When I went up there I drove Touchy's car. When I come out the place after the cops had pushed me around and searched me and everything, Carlos was there getting the car. I asked him what he was doing there and he just told me to give him Touchy's car keys. Then he split. I figured Touchy must have set me up because of what you done."

"Because of what *I* did?"

"Hey, look, I know I been jiving around." Tony looked away. "I really don't need to hear it."

A doctor came out, looking younger than Didi wanted a doctor to look, and told them that their mother was resting comfortably.

"She's asleep now, and I'd like to have her get some rest. We've given her a mild sedative and something to bring her pressure down. She'll probably be better off if you don't see her until tomorrow. You can come visit her anytime after twelve."

"Is she going to be okay?" Didi asked.

"I think so," the doctor said. "The danger in this kind of case is not the stroke, because I think that this was really a very mild one. I think the problem is that there could be future strokes as well. Her blood pressure is really high and her blood workup shows some signs of kidney involvement. We'll keep her here a few days and then put her on a good after-care program."

That night Tony tried to kick his habit cold turkey, but by eleven he was sick. He took what money he had and hit the streets, looking for something to stop the pain, telling himself lies that even he didn't believe. He got some dope from a guy in Peewee's Bar up on 147th Street and also some methadone from a guy he met who owed him a favor.

The next day it was Reggie that found Tony. Reggie had some dope with him, enough to fix Tony up for the day, but Tony was afraid of it.

"I don't know what's wrong with you," Reggie said. "You sure can use some fixing."

"I don't need nothing," Tony said. They were standing in front of his house.

"Yeah, look, Touchy said he wanted you to know that he was sorry for what happened. He think he got a rat in the organization."

"Yeah, I bet he do," Tony said. "If he got a rat in the organization he must be changing his own name to Mousey."

"You got to send that right in to Bob Hope," Reggie said, a sneer lifting his top lip. "Maybe he'll think it's funny."

"I didn't think what happened to me was funny, either," Tony said. His stomach was beginning to cramp.

"You know, Touchy wants somebody to take care of that Motown dude. Make it look like an accident. I figured maybe you and me do the job. Touchy pay five hundred dollars."

"Why don't you cop a walk?" Tony said.

"Watch your mouth," Reggie said. "I don't take but so much lip 'fore I got to cut somebody."

"Hey, you feel froggy, just come on and leap over here,"

Tony said. "I ain't scared of you, and that's stone the word."

By the time Reggie left Tony felt really sick. His stomach was upset, and he was as down as he could get. But even more than that, he was sick because he realized that the only thing he could think of, more than his mother being in the hospital, more than what Touchy had done to him, was about getting a fix. That was what it was about now. He was part of the subway map that Touchy was always talking about.

"Man, this whole area is nothing but a big subway map," Touchy had said. "Full of veins and arteries just waiting for what I got to sell. And every junkie out there is just another stop along the way."

Well, Tony might be just another stop, but he was going to let everybody know that Touchy was working with the Man. That's just what I'm going to do, he thought.

He went uptown again and spent his last money. He felt bad but he still waited until he got home before getting himself straight.

Didi hadn't seen her brother all day. She had hoped that he would go to the hospital with her. When she got there she found her mother sitting up in bed, looking tired but not too bad. Her color was wrong, though—her normally vibrant brown skin looked dull. She was being cared for by a few older black nurses and a young Irish girl, no older than Didi, in a trainee's uniform. Darlene asked about Tony, and Didi lied, saying that he'd gone out and got some "piece of job" and would be up to see her that night.

Her mother said that that was the way men were.

"Always needing a job so they can buy their freedom," she had said.

Now there he was, half-nodding-out, half-awake, eating a candy bar in front of the television set. She didn't want to deal with it. She just wanted to walk away, to shut him out of her mind.

"What's happening, Sis?" Tony's words were slurred.

"You know, if Motown hadn't taken the stuff away from you, you might be in jail today," Didi said. "You ought to have thanked him."

"Somebody better thank him in a hurry," Tony said. "Touchy's mad. Reggie told me."

"What—?" Didi cut herself off. There wasn't any use in talking to Tony. There wasn't any use in talking to him or all the hollow people like him. But she owed Motown something. She would go and talk to him, tell him what Tony had said. She'd think about it first, then talk to him later.

The hospital was so cold, so unwelcoming, but Darlene Johnson looked better. She was sitting up. Mrs. Lucas, an old friend of the family, had brought her a new housecoat. Its white and pink collar formed a soft halo of bright fabric around her mother's head.

"I feel all right, really," Darlene was saying.

She looked fresh, better than Didi had seen her look in years. Her skin glowed with color. Didi thought that her mother must have been a fine-looking woman at one time.

"They gave me so many tests I don't know what to do. Every time I turned around they was taking some blood or something. I guess they know what they doing."

"You just keep doing what they tell you to, Mama," Didi said. "You'll be up and around before you even know it."

"Mrs. Lucas came," Darlene Johnson went on, "and I sure was surprised . . ."

Didi listened as her mother talked about how Mrs. Lucas and the nurses seemed to care for her. She was surprised that the little things they did had meant so much to her mother, and wished that she had done some of them herself.

". . . now you make sure that Tony eats. You know how he is, always ready to cut and run. Now you make sure he eats, Didi."

"Yes, ma'am." Didi kissed her mother's cheek and patted her thin hand.

What do you feel? Didi asked herself. It bothered her, she knew. There were things going on inside of her that she did not want to feel. There were thoughts that kept coming to her mind, pushing themselves into her head, mocking her.

No matter what happened, her mother wouldn't get any easier to deal with; she would be harder. Didi would have to spend more time with her. She would have to give more of herself, and she wasn't sure she had any more to give. To give meant being here and now, being flesh and blood, and reaching out to touch other flesh and blood and other heres and nows. But somehow Didi had put her heres and nows away from her. This was not what she wanted. She did not think of herself as just Didi Johnson who lived in Harlem, but as the Didi Johnson she would become years from now. The years in between would bring college and choices, so many choices, so many people she could be.

When Didi Johnson walked down the street and some slick dude would drop his, "Hey, baby, I sure would like to . . . ," he would be talking to a dream he was having, not to her. When she woke in the mornings and saw the sun through the cracked pane of her window, it was not the real Didi seeing it, but someone the real Didi would soon leave behind.

Her mother needed her now. That was real, even though she knew it was a trap. For any person she cared for, any brick in the squatting buildings that she touched, any rhythm she walked to in the streets would help to trap her in Harlem.

It was almost dark, much too late to go up the stairs of the building Motown lived in. What could be up there? But if she didn't go and something happened to him, she would feel terrible. No, she would do it. She would run into the building and tell him that Touchy was out to get him. Quickly, before it got too dark.

She looked around and waited until she was sure that no one could see her enter the building. If someone saw, some wino, some junkie, some fiend, they might follow her. She waited, and looked and then went in.

The smell was bad. It seemed worse, even, than it had before. There was a scurrying in the dark. She stopped. Her heart was racing. She listened. Nothing. She took another step and stopped again. Had she heard more scurrying? Were they rats? Some furry animal moving faster than she thought possible along the uneven floor? Did it have small red eyes?

"Motown!"

Nothing. She turned and started to go back down the few steps she had managed. What was that? Had she heard something behind the door on the first floor?

"Motown!"

"Who down there?"

"It's me, Didi."

A circle of light fell before her. It was his flashlight. She went up the stairs, following the light that he held before her. She went behind him into his place. He closed the door and turned on another light. She saw that the window was covered over with a blanket so that no one could see the light from the outside. With the two lights that he had lit, both kerosene lamps, the room was quite bright.

The room hadn't changed. In a corner wastebasket there was a crumpled bag from Chicken Delight. There was a book on the table. Something by Dumas. She hadn't thought that he would be a reader.

"I thought I'd better tell you something," she said.

"Like what?" He looked down, away from her.

"Tony said you took some dope from him," Didi said.

"I didn't want . . ." He didn't finish the sentence. For a moment they stood, the silence between them, both of them feeling awkward.

"I thought you were doing it to help him," Didi said.

"I was." Motown looked up at her.

"I know," Didi said, taking a step closer to him and then, catching herself, stopping. "I know."

"Them people he be with ain't no . . . aren't no good," Motown said. "They use that dope and stuff."

"Why do you involve yourself?" Didi asked. "I mean, you don't have to or anything, but—"

"I just do."

"Why?" Didi asked. Wondering why she just didn't tell him what she had come for and leave.

" 'Cause he's either my people needing my help," Motown said, shrugging, "or he ain't."

"I don't understand."

"You want a soda?"

"You have a soda?"

"I just bought some," Motown said. "You can sit down if you want to."

Didi looked around. There was a wooden chair and the bed. She sat on the chair. Motown took two sodas from a box. When he pulled the box out from a corner and took off the lid, Didi saw that it was full of ice. There was a container of milk in the box as well. Both of the sodas were orange, and he gave her one. He sat on the edge of the bed.

"How did you know that Tony was going to be up there?" Didi asked.

"You know Reggie? Got a long head?"

"Hangs out with Touchy sometimes?"

"Yeah, that's him," Motown said. "Anyway, he said that Tony was going to be up there. He said he was going to be driving Touchy's car. I just figured he was getting into some more dope business, until I went up there and seen things wasn't right. I didn't even know that Tony was messing around with that stuff—not serious, anyway."

"He's serious."

"I'm sorry," Motown said.

"Yes." Didi looked at Motown, knowing that he meant what he said, wondering about it. "Tony said that he heard Touchy was going to try to get even with you for what you did."

"He mad at me?" Motown asked. "I mean Tony, he mad at me?"

"I think the only thing he's interested in right now is drugs," Didi said. "You know, I don't even want to say it. I don't want to even think about my brother being a junkie."

"I didn't think you did," Motown said. "You more of a schoolgirl than a street people. But that's okay."

"I guess so," she said.

He looked at her and down at the floor. There was an old piece of linoleum on the floor with a floral design. The linoleum was cracked and chipped over the uneven floorboards.

"You don't think much of me, do you?" Didi said.

"Yeah, I do," Motown said. "I like you."

"That why you have to look at the floor when you say it?" Didi asked.

"I like you," Motown said, looking up at Didi.

She held his eyes for a while and then he smiled. It was a good, warm smile that caught her by surprise. She smiled back and quickly they both looked away from each other.

"Look, what are you going to do about Touchy?" Didi asked, changing the tone of her voice and telling herself that she was getting back to business and only glancing at Motown.

"Nothing to do," Motown said. "I mean, if he going to try to mess with me, I just have to get myself ready."

"You're not going to stay here, are you?" Didi asked. "I don't know if he knows you live here, but somebody around here probably does."

"I'll stay here," Motown said. "Might as well."

"Look, I have a few dollars, not much, but—"

"I have money," Motown said. He reached behind the cot and pulled out his bankbook and threw it on the table in front of Didi.

"I don't want to see your bankbook," Didi said, wanting to see it.

"I'll stay here," Motown said.

Didi sat quietly for a minute, then picked up Motown's bankbook and looked at it.

"Frank," she said. "I like that name."

"My friends call me Motown," he answered.

"I didn't know you had this much money," Didi said, surprised. "It's not a world, but it's okay. It's really okay."

"I'm trying to save up enough to get another place," Motown answered. "A regular place. But I don't want to move in if I got to move out right away because I ain't got the money to stay."

"If you have this much money, I think you should move now," Didi said. "You could get a small place, maybe a room with a little kitchen on one end of it. You've seen that kind of place?"

"Yeah."

"It'd be better than living here," Didi said. "Especially with the trouble with Touchy. I could help you fix it up."

"Yeah?" Motown said.

"I saw some places over on a Hundred Twenty-second, near Morningside," Didi said. "If I'm over there again I'll check them out for you."

"Okay," Motown said.

When she left, Motown couldn't do anything except sit on the edge of the bed and stare at the door. It wasn't that he knew anything about her, because he didn't. He knew that she was Tony's sister. He knew that she didn't like the streets much, but that was all. Still, she had come into the room and somehow filled it with her presence. There was a way that she had of holding her head at an angle so that it looked as if she was seeing things in a way that Motown didn't know how they looked. He wanted to be in her eyes, looking out on the world, seeing what she saw, thinking about what she had seen.

No, that wasn't it. It was the way she held her hands together in front of her bosom, as if she was holding herself in. As if she was, perhaps, waiting for just some right time to do something.

His book had been on the table, never mind that he hadn't gotten around to reading it yet. She had seen his bankbook. It wasn't the world, she had said, but still she had been impressed.

Motown was surprised the way he acted around Didi.

Usually he wouldn't have let anyone see his bankbook. He wouldn't have cared if anyone saw him reading the books that the Professor gave him, either. It was better that way, he felt. He knew that if his parents had lived things would have been different. He wouldn't have had to go to all the foster homes, always staying on the edge of somebody else's life.

Motown thought about Mrs. Dodson, remembering how the people at the Institute had said that she would be good for him. They said that she was a kind woman who didn't take any nonsense, and if she took Motown, everything would be just right between them because they were the same kind of people. He remembered lying on his cot at the Institute when the word came that he would be going to Mrs. Dodson's that weekend. He had been told that she taught piano, and he imagined himself learning the piano and playing for her. She would look at him and say that he had done well.

On the night that he dreamt these things it had snowed and the wind howled outside the windows of the Institute and rattled the front doors down the long, pale green hall. For some reason, known only to God and the secret voices within him, he had thought that things would work out between him and Mrs. Dodson. And they did for a long time. It took Mrs. Dodson nearly two years, even with the money she got from the Institute, to buy the house she wanted. It was, she was fond of saying, her social security.

"If you don't look out for yourself, ain't nobody gonna look out for you, boy," she said. "You remember that."

That was the last thing she told him before the people

from the Institute came and picked him up, because Mrs. Dodson was no longer interested in keeping a foster child.

It was also the last time that Motown had trusted another human being completely. But then, he hadn't met Didi Johnson.

He didn't want to trust Didi Johnson. He didn't say to himself, ever, that Didi Johnson was a person to trust, or even that she was okay. But the way she held her hands, and the way she smiled, and the way she put her long legs out in front of herself and crossed them at the ankles, kept coming back to him. No, they wouldn't leave him.

Frank Motown Williams was down to two dollars and forty-seven cents. He had told himself that he was going to take twenty dollars out of the bank the next day. But now he didn't want to. He wanted Didi to see that he put money in the bank. He thought about Touchy, about what he might do, but he wasn't worried.

In the morning he would look again for a job. Anything would do, he thought, as long as he didn't have to take money from the bank. He lay back on the bed and tried to relax, but couldn't. The girl excited him. She did things to him that he couldn't fight against, and there, all alone and framed by the cracked plaster, and the forever-old linoleum, and the boarded-up window, and the ancient, yellowed door, he smiled a broad, silly smile.

Motown got up later than he had planned. It was nearly nine by the time he had gotten the A train and taken it down to the World Trade Center at Chambers Street. The bathroom near the PATH trains to New Jersey was the best kept in the city. He went into it and washed quickly, rinsing his mouth out with a mixture of salt and peroxide from a bottle that he kept for that purpose. It had cost him ninety cents to get to the World Trade Center. It cost another fifty cents to take the PATH train to Jersey City. He got there and walked the one mile from the station to the place where they bought blood for nine dollars a pint.

"You don't take no drugs or nothing like that?" the young Puerto Rican girl asked him.

Motown shook his head no.

"You got any diseases?"

Again, no.

"Go to booth four. After you give blood you can get some free orange juice." She had great, dark eyes and a wide mouth. "Only it's not really orange juice, it's Tang."

"That's okay," Motown said.

He gave blood, collected his nine dollars, and then went to Fourteenth Street to see if he could get a job.

CHAPTER V

IT WAS A SILLY FEELING, SHE TOLD HERSELF. EVEN AFTER she had talked with the small brown-skinned lady renting kitchenettes on Eighth Avenue and had put ten dollars on the week's rent.

"How long have you been married?" the frail woman had asked. "You don't look more than a baby."

"Oh, the apartment's not for me," Didi had said. "It's

for . . . my cousin. He just came up from North Carolina and we don't have a place for him."

The woman hadn't believed her. There was distrust in the sad eyes that looked up at Didi.

"You look so familiar," the woman had said. "Do you live around here?"

"No, ma'am," Didi had answered. The room was small but bright and clean. There was a pull-out cot against the wall, a small table, a tiny refrigerator, and two gas burners that were somehow hooked up on the side of the sink.

"You're not one of those Jehovah Witness ladies, are you? Not that I have anything against them, you know."

"I go to Bethel," Didi answered. At least her mother went to Bethel.

"That's where I've seen you," Mrs. Robinson said, pointing her finger at Didi. "We went on a picnic with Bethel about two or three years ago. That's where I must have seen you."

The woman's attitude changed. The sad eyes looked less sad as she showed Didi where her "cousin" could keep his pots and pans under the sink.

But it didn't mean anything, Didi told herself as she left. If she had cared for Motown, that is, cared for him more than having a vague liking for the way he looked and the fact that he had helped both herself and her brother, things might have been different. She might have liked the idea of finding a place for him, and of imagining him there. She shrugged as she reached the subway. The place was small, but it was better than the one that Motown was staying in.

It was a piece of a job, nothing that he wanted. He was hired at the Caravel Cleaners on East Sixty-eighth Street.

"You pick up and deliver," Mrs. Mott said. "When you're not picking up or delivering, you keep the back clean. I don't want you out front. You understand that?"

Motown understood. He was a delivery boy. He hated that kind of job. What had the Professor said? "If you got the kind of job where you can't learn anything, you're paying extra just to keep it."

But it was a job. It paid one hundred and sixty dollars a week and whatever Mrs. Mott meant by occasional tips. She had said, too, that she'd had three or four boys in the last month, and "they don't seem to want to stay."

At first he had told Mrs. Mott that he would think about the job, but when Didi had told him about the apartment, he knew he would take it.

"It's fifty dollars a week, but you don't have to pay gas and electric," she had said.

He had never had too good a job, or too steady a job either, and the rent scared him a little. Fifty dollars a week wasn't bad but you still had to get it up every week, he thought. He didn't have any furniture to put into an apartment either. It was better, he knew, when you had your own furniture.

But that wasn't the major reason that Motown hadn't rented his own apartment before. One of the things he had always had, in all the buildings that he had lived in, was the idea that it wasn't permanent. That somehow things would change in his life and the walls wouldn't groan in loneliness in the middle of the night and the floors wouldn't creak their complaints to the darkness and he would have somebody to live with. He would dream how it would come about in a hundred ways. Perhaps he would be walking down the street, down Lenox Avenue, and he'd see a tall man, black as Motown, no, blacker still. As black as the ebony statues that stood on the shelves in the back of the Professor's shop, leaning on their sticks, guarding the knowledge of Africa that sprawled about them. And this tall man, this tall black man would come walking down Lenox Avenue and see him and call to him.

"What's your name, boy?" he would say. His voice would be deep, like distant thunder, yet gentle.

"Motown," he would answer.

"No, I mean what name were you born with?"

Then Motown would look into the stranger's face and would have to catch his breath, for the man looked just like him.

"Frank Williams," Motown would say.

"I've been looking for you all these years," the man would say. "I am your father and you are my son."

And they would embrace and the man would take Motown with him and they would have a place together. That's what it was all about, having a place together with someone. A father, come from the hidden darkness of the past, or perhaps a friend.

He had met a boy once, a young boy with wide eyes

who had run away from home. He had told the boy that he couldn't stay with him in a place he had near St. Nicholas Avenue. And later, when the boy had left, Motown had cried himself to sleep.

It wasn't no big thing. When a man became a warrior he had to go into the house of his father and call upon the spirits of all the fathers that had gone before him. And then he would have to sit in the darkness alone and wait for the spirits to guide him. That was what the Professor said that young men did in Africa when they came of age. Being alone was part of being a man.

"I can put them up," Motown said, watching Didi as she teetered on the chair adjusting the curtains she had bought.

"They're okay, now," Didi said. She hopped off the chair and stood back to see her handiwork. "Not bad, what do you think?"

"I like them," Motown said.

"They'll look even better when the sun shines through them," Didi said. "I think this place will be really cozy after a while. You really like it?"

"Yeah," Motown said. They had worked all morning on fixing it up.

"I got these with my Washington money," Didi said, producing some curtains from a shopping bag she had brought with her. "I got the dishes from my house. We have more dishes than the Five and Ten."

"What's your Washington money?"

"Money I was going to take with me when I went away to college," Didi said. "I had a part-time job during the year with the school board. You like the curtains?"

"Yeah, they're nice," Motown answered.

"Now what you need is a radio, or maybe a record player," Didi said. "You can buy one of those small ones. You don't need anything big, really."

"Maybe."

"Maybe?" Didi looked at him. "You don't really like the place, do you?"

"I like it," Motown said. There was a cabinet under the sink and Motown had bought a small can of paint to cover the inside of it. He bent forward to reach the corners.

"If you like it, why are you so quiet?" Didi asked. She knelt beside him on the floor. "If this was my place I'd be so happy I'd be hopping around."

"I'm happy," Motown said. "I just don't know what to say, I guess."

"Tell me what you like about it," Didi said.

"I like the way it looks." Motown dipped the brush in the white paint, held it over the can for a moment while the excess dripped off, and then ran the brush along the base of the cabinet so that the paint would drip into the cracks and seal it from roaches.

"How come men can never say what they mean?" Didi asked. "I was hoping that you would be as happy about this place as I am."

"I'm happy because you like it," Motown said. "That's a big part of it."

"You're happy because *I* like it?" Didi turned sideways and sat on the freshly scrubbed linoleum floor. "That's no reason for—"

Suddenly she knew. She looked at him, watched as he finished dabbing the brush into a corner of the cabinet, and then stood up.

"If you thought," she said, gathering up her things, "for one minute that I helped you to get this place because I had some kind of *thing* for you, then you're wrong."

"I didn't say that," Motown said. "I didn't say that you had some kind of thing for me."

"Good," Didi said. "Let's leave it that way."

"That would be real bad, huh?" Motown covered the paint can carefully. "If you had some kind of . . . what did you say? Some kind of *thing* for me?"

"Look, Motown, I've got a lot of things to do with my life," Didi said. She had her things gathered and was ready to leave. "I really appreciate your helping me out, and I don't even think that me helping you to find this place is the same thing. But it doesn't mean that I like you except as a friend. You know, too many girls get themselves all wrapped up in some guy and before you know it there are places like this and a stomach full of babies. I want more than that."

"Okay," Motown said.

"I don't want to hurt you, Motown." Didi looked down at where he still sat in front of the cabinet. "Can you understand that?"

"Yeah," Motown said. "It ain't no big thing."

Touchy didn't like going to see Mr. Bell. Bell, in his early forties, owned one of the dimly lit stores on Forty-second Street that specialized in off-color books, tapes, and live peep shows in the back. Bell didn't want Touchy or anyone else parking in front of his place and attracting attention, so Touchy had to park on Ninth Avenue and walk to the Garden of Pleasures.

"I don't know." Bell puffed on a big cigar and blew smoke in short puffs toward the ceiling. "From what I hear, you can't handle what you got, let alone take care of more business."

"I can handle as much business as there is out there," Touchy said. "I don't see why you thinking about bringing in anybody else. It don't make any sense to me."

"It makes sense to me," Bell said, " 'cause I hear you can't even control your own people."

"I don't have any control problems," Touchy said. "Some stupid chick went over to the precinct, but I got that straight."

"That's not what I hear," Bell said. "I heard you were trying to set somebody up and that didn't go down either."

Touchy looked at Bell. He was about five-five, maybe five-six at most. The impression was of a little man trying to be a big man. He wore a large diamond ring on his little finger, his cigar was big—even his clothes seemed too big for him.

"Then you talking to the wrong people," Touchy said, wondering just who Bell was getting his information from. "I know my business."

"No, you don't know this business," Bell said. "I know this business, but you don't. You think you can play it on both sides of the street, but you can't. You're one of these guys that need people to like you. So you walk around and show everybody your teeth and try to get somebody to take a light fall. But what you're doing is stupid, see? 'Cause even if the fall goes down the way you planned it, it don't mean nothing. Some junkie goes to jail, big deal. So you figure everybody is going to say it ain't your fault and they're still gonna love you. I got news for you, baby. The only one's gonna love you is the junkies when they see you with their stuff. And the first time they get a chance, they're gonna put a hurting on you. You can't put dope in the streets and expect people to like you. If you need them to like you, then you're in the wrong business. You got to care more for the money than for the garbage that lives up there, because even garbage don't like to get messed over."

"They ain't all garbage," Touchy said. "The junkies are the garbage. They ain't worth two cents."

"They wasn't born garbage," Bell said. "And if it wasn't for beauties like you, sweetheart, they wouldn't be junkies today."

"Hey, look, man, you don't act like you care to do business with me, either."

"This ain't a caring business, Touchy. Now why don't you run along and figure out what you want to do."

"Yeah," Touchy said. "Right."

"Hey, you want some dirty books?"

Touchy didn't answer.

CHAPTER VI

THE LETTER FROM THE UNIVERSITY OF WISCONSIN ARRIVED on the third of July. Didi had forgotten about Wisconsin. She had sent off the application the year before but hadn't heard anything about it except that she was being considered. She read the letter twice. It was a scholarship offer. They would give her a partial scholarship, which meant that she wouldn't have to pay tuition or for her books, and if she wanted them to, they would try to arrange a job for her that would meet the costs of the dormitory and other expenses. They regretted having contacted her so late, but their minority recruiting program was only recently clarified.

"So what else it say?" Darlene asked her daughter.

"That's all," Didi said. "Except to let them know if I wasn't going to take the scholarship so they could offer it to someone else."

"So what are you going to do?" her mother asked.

"Do?" Didi asked, the tears already welling in her eyes. "What do you mean?"

"You got to make up your mind right away?" Mrs. Johnson turned her head toward the wall. "The doctor said that if I had another accident I might die. Then I wouldn't need you so much, baby."

"Mama, you're not going to die," Didi said.

"Okay," her mother said, rising up to lean on one elbow, "then I guess you'd better go, then."

"Mama?"

"Don't cry, baby." Darlene Johnson patted her daughter's hand. "You just do what you have to do."

"Mama, I feel so messed around." Didi put her head down on her mother's shoulder. "If I stay here and go to school at night, it's going to take me five, maybe six years to finish. I just don't know if I can do it. All during high school I kept telling myself that I was going to college and imagining how it would be. I watch the football games on television and I don't even look at the players, I look at the kids in the stands. That's what I want to do, be one of those kids in the stands. I just don't want to be here anymore."

"You saying it's hard, girl?" Her mother lifted her head and looked into her face. "You look at me with those pretty brown eyes and tell me that you think it's hard, baby."

"Mama, you might have had it harder, but for me it's hard now. It's so hard." The sobs choked her, caught her words in her throat and strangled them. She picked up a dishtowel and wiped her face with it.

"It's hard because you're such a decent child, baby," Darlene said. "You want so much and you dream so big. God, but you can dream so big. When you and Tony was little and your father had just gone, I used to think that I'd raise you both real good just to spite your father—show him I didn't need him. That's what I used to think. Only I thought it more about Tony than I did you. Because deep inside I think that I felt if I raised him good, if I made him into something special, then your father would be proud of me. Ain't that something? Me sitting in my kitchen crying my eyes out because the man left me alone, and the only thing I'm thinking about is what I can do to make him think I'm something good again? Ain't that something? I never did think too much of how you would turn out. Not that I didn't love you, because as God is my secret judge, I sure did and I sure do now. I just never thought you would grow up to dream so big.

"Tony, he throwing his life away with that dope and you here with your heart breaking trying to hold the family together. Sometimes I try to think of what went wrong, but the more I think on it the less come to me."

"You know about Tony?"

"I've seen good boys go down that road before, but it never hurt as much as when I seen Tony start. You know I can't hardly speak on it now without . . ."

Her voice trailed off and she looked away.

The last person that messed with Tutmose, as far as anybody knew, was Billy Samples. Billy had told some girl how he was going to trick Tutmose out of a dollar, and when he couldn't, he got mad and punched Tutmose on the side of his face. Tutmose backed against the wall and Billy waded in with both fists flying. Tutmose caught Billy around his waist and threw him down and wouldn't let him up. They rolled around with Billy trying to punch the best he could and Tutmose squeezing as hard as he could. Then Billy broke free and punched Tutmose in the face, and Tutmose punched back and the fight was over. Tutmose couldn't do much in the way of boxing, but he could hit like a Georgia mule kicks. Not only that, but after they finally got Tutmose off Billy, the fight still didn't end. Every time that Tutmose saw Billy, night or day, the fight would start again. Tutmose hadn't understood why Billy should fight him in the first place, so didn't need a reason to start fighting whenever he saw him from then on.

So when Touchy told Reggie he would give him three hundred dollars to "take care of" Motown and Reggie wanted to let Motown know about it, he approached Motown's friend Tutmose very carefully.

"Hey, Tutmose, what's happening?" Reggie started to lean against the building, then thought better of it.

"Got a new newspaper," Tutmose said. "It only costs a quarter. Only paper around got color in it."

"You see Motown around?"

"Sometime he be around," Tutmose said. "Why, you looking for him?"

"Yeah, you see him you tell him that I'm looking for him," Reggie said. "Tell him I got an extra head-whippin' and I think he could use it."

"Why you want to mess with Motown for?" Tutmose asked, folding some newspapers into neat thirds to hand to people coming from the subway. "He don't mess with nobody."

"He got a bad habit of putting his nose into people's business," Reggie said. "I'm gonna see to it that he stops that."

"I don't see why you got to mess with—"

Reggie walked away. He knew that Tutmose would tell

Motown when he saw him. If Tutmose told him that Reggie was going to beat him up, it would throw Motown off. He hadn't really checked Motown out in the hallway. He was messing with the chick and Motown had sneaked up on him. But from what little action there was, he knew that Motown was strong, and he knew he had a lot of heart. He didn't want to fight him in a stand-up, street-corner kind of thing. That wasn't what Touchy wanted anyway.

"The dude's messing with my reputation," Touchy had said. "When I walk the streets, people supposed to respect my footsteps."

"He ain't nothing," Reggie said. "He just a junior bum. I think the dude's a head case, too."

"Yeah, well I want you to make him a box case. You think you can handle the weight?"

"Yeah, I can handle it," Reggie said.

"Why don't you go over to the Sunset and get you a piece?" Touchy said. "Buy it, don't rent the sucker. Then throw it down the sewer some place when you done."

Reggie had never killed anybody before, but he didn't think it would be a big thing, not with a piece. He did like Touchy said, went over to the Sunset Bar and Grill and bought a piece from Prez for sixty-five dollars. Touchy had given him two hundred and fifty dollars for the job, with a promise of another two fifty when it was done. The gun was loaded when he got it from Prez, and everything was sweet. But then he had gone to where he thought Motown was staying and tried to figure out how he was going to get him out. There was no way he was going to go into an old building in the dark. That's when he found out that Motown had moved, and the chick had either moved in with him or had just helped him to move. That made Reggie kind of nervous. The talk on the street was that Touchy had set up Tony for the Man to bust 'cause he owed the Man a favor. Motown had seen to it that Tony got away clean. Now he wondered if Touchy wasn't giving him up. Otherwise how would Motown know to move?

Reggie figured he'd sound on Motown and see what he knew. If he didn't know how serious the action was, he would just run his mouth or try something with his hands. Then Reggie would waste him. If he knew something, he'd be carrying a pipe or maybe a knife. Motown wasn't the kind of dude to carry a gun, and even if he had one, he wasn't the kind of guy to blow somebody away unless he had to. But the more Reggie thought about it, the more he knew that he really couldn't figure out Motown at all. He lived like a bum, but if Tony's sister was helping him to make his move, he must have something going for him. The girl was a fox and a schoolgirl, so Reggie couldn't see what she saw in Motown.

One of the things that Motown hadn't thought about at the dry cleaner's job was how hot it would be. The outside, where the customers came to leave or pick up clothing, was air-conditioned, but the back, where the presser worked and where the clothes were hung, was not. The heat and the smell of the spotting fluid drained him. By quitting time he was hardly able to stand. He couldn't have stood it at all if it weren't for the times when he was out delivering clothing. It was the kind of job that he hated, but he knew that everyone else would, too, and he could keep it for probably as long as he wanted to. He thought about keeping it for a year, to see how much money he could save. Then if he could save enough he'd take a day off now and then and look for something else. That way he would, at least, be able to keep the apartment.

What had happened with Didi had been bad. He hadn't really put it into words. But when he saw Didi, when she was anywhere near him, he felt funny. It was almost embarrassing. He had been around other girls before, some just about as good-looking as Didi, and he had never felt the way he did around her. Then, when she said that there wasn't anything going on between them, it hurt. It had hurt bad, even though he hadn't ever thought that there *was* anything going on more than the way he felt.

He checked his keys, the way he did a hundred times a day. The keys meant something to him. Once he had been on Forty-second Street and saw an old drunk stop a nun walking down the street. The nun was in the kind of black robelike thing that nuns wore sometimes, and she had a large crucifix around her neck. The bum started calling her names and saying how she wasn't any good, and all the while the nun just looked at him and twisted the cross with her fingers. It meant a lot to her, it did, and his keys meant something like that to him. It was the first time in his life that he had his own place, that he wasn't sleeping somewhere that he might have to move from the next day, or that he would be afraid to like because it belonged to someone else. Didi had changed all of that. She had expected something different and she had just done it, like it wasn't supposed to be the way he'd been doing it.

Some Muslims were selling incense on the corner. He didn't like incense even though the Professor often burned it in his shop.

"When Noah came down from the ark onto dry land," the Professor said, "he offered a sacrifice of sweet-smelling herbs unto the Lord, and the Lord was pleased."

Some other brothers were selling African-like carvings, and Motown thought that when he had got a little ahead on his savings, he might buy one or two and put them around his place.

He thought of some other things he wanted to do, too. He would build a bookcase and buy some books from the Professor. The Professor! He hadn't thought much about him since he had moved. He would invite the Professor to his house for dinner. He had often been to the Professor's house for the simple meals the old man would prepare. Now he could return the invitation. Motown's thoughts wandered to the Professor and what he would have when the Professor came to dinner. He would have to learn to cook, too. It didn't seem like a hard thing to do. He had already made rice and cooked frankfurters by boiling them. Maybe he could get a frying pan and learn to fry up some chicken.

"Hello."

Didi's voice startled Motown. He looked up and saw her sitting on the steps. She wore dark slacks and a white sleeveless blouse.

"Hi." Motown stood and looked up at her.

"I had some bad news today," Didi said. "I guess I didn't feel like staying home, so I thought I'd come over to see what you were doing. You just getting in from work?"

"Yeah," Motown said, wondering how best to talk to this girl. "You want to go for some coffee or something? Maybe a soda?"

"I brought one of my mother's frying pans over and some hamburger," Didi said. "Thought maybe I'd make you supper, if you haven't eaten. Have you?"

"No," Motown said. "What's the bad news?"

"I'll tell you upstairs," Didi said.

They got upstairs and Motown looked around to see how the place looked. Not bad. There was a T-shirt on the back of a chair and he took that and put it in a pillowcase he kept for his dirty clothes. He opened a window as Didi took the hamburger from the bag.

"I got an offer for a scholarship out to the University of Wisconsin today," Didi said.

"That's sounds good," Motown said.

"Did I tell you my mother's sick?"

"No," Motown said. "You didn't tell me anything about your mother, or much about anything else."

"She's sick," Didi said. "She really can't take care of herself too tough. She's always had this thing that she's been—kind of mixed up, I guess you'd call it. Then she had a little stroke. You know what a stroke is?"

"I seen people who had them," Motown said.

"Well, she's not that bad," Didi said. She had taken the hamburger and pounded it flat with the palm of her hand. Then she diced an onion she had brought with her and sprinkled that over the hamburger. "You have any eggs?"

"In the refrigerator," Motown said, glad that he had the eggs.

"With her sick and Tony screwing up his life at a great rate, I just wouldn't feel right going off to Wisconsin, even though I would really like to go," Didi said. She cracked an egg into a jar that Motown had on the shelf, and then began to mix the egg into the hamburger and onion. "You know, as soon as I saw the letter I began to feel bad. I just want—you ever want something really bad?"

"Lots of things," Motown said.

"I bet you never wanted anything as bad as I wanted to go away to college."

"Probably not," Motown said.

The corn oil was the same bottle that Didi had brought when she first helped Motown set up the small apartment. She looked to see how much of it he had used and saw that he hadn't used any.

"What's the thing you wanted most?" Didi asked. "The apartment?"

"I don't know." Motown thought about his answer for a moment. "A brother, maybe."

"Oh." Didi turned and looked at Motown for a long moment, then turned back to the hamburgers. She put some of the oil in the pan, turned on the flame, and let it get hot as she shaped the hamburger.

"What was the bad news?" Motown asked.

"That was it," Didi said, "the fact that I can't go away to school."

"You going to go to college in New York now?"

"I don't want to, but maybe I will if it's between that and no college at all," Didi said, adjusting the flame. "In fact, I'm sure I'll try to do something."

"I thought the bad news was something about Tony," Motown said.

"Why?" Didi asked.

"I didn't think, after the other time, that you'd come back here again," Motown said.

"I . . ." Didi took a deep breath. "You know, I didn't even think about what I said the other day. I just need to be away from my house and I thought of . . . Motown, I'm sorry."

"I'm not," Motown said. "I'm just glad to see you again."

"Oh, you're so sweet," Didi said. "You really are."

She went over to him and kissed him lightly on the cheek as he sat on the bed.

"You know," she said, returning to the hamburgers, "if you were standing up I could just about reach you if I wanted to kiss you on the mouth."

"How you know that?" Motown asked.

"I was just thinking about it," Didi said. "I mean I wasn't thinking about it, but it came to me."

"I'm not that tall," Motown said. "And even if I was, I'd bend over if you ever want to kiss me."

Didi turned away quickly and took a knife and turned the hamburgers. She told herself that she really didn't want to get into anything with Motown. She had thought about kissing him though, wondering if he would have to bend over. She imagined herself reaching up to his lips, perhaps even getting up on her toes. He had pretty eyes, and if he kept his eyes open, she would keep hers open as well.

"So how is Tony?"

"He's about the same," Didi said. "He's telling himself that he's cool. He said he used to have a problem, but now he's cutting back. I don't know, he might be. What do you think?"

"You sticking stuff in your veins that ain't supposed to be there," Motown said, "you ain't cool."

The hamburgers were browned on one side, and Didi turned them over again.

"I think that as long as I'm around there's a chance he'll deal with it," Didi said. "Even if he's lying sometimes about having a problem, at least he's trying to deal with it on some level. You know what I mean?"

"People got so much to deal with," Motown said. "It's hard trying to deal with all of it at once."

"That's it." Didi turned back toward Motown. "You know why I want to go away to college? Because I don't want to deal with everything around here. I don't want to have to go to school and study and then come home and have to deal with winos in the street. I don't want to have to deal with my brother using dope. I just want to deal with going to school and thinking about what I want to do with the rest of my life. Don't you ever feel that way?"

"Mostly I just think about what I'm going to be doing from one day to the next," Motown said. "Sometimes I think about what the people around here are doing. This guy I know, I call him the Professor—I get books from him—sometimes we talk about how you see people doing things and they look like they're doing one thing and they're really doing something else."

"Like what?" Didi asked.

"Like they using dope and they saying it makes them feel good, only what they really doing is killing themselves."

"If they put enough of that stuff into them they'll either kill themselves with an overdose or get killed robbing somebody to buy more," Didi said. "You don't see old drug addicts on the street."

"No, that's not what I'm talking about," Motown said. "You're talking about how your body is, that kind of being dead. I'm talking about the other way. Like you said that you want to go away to college, right?"

"Yeah, go on."

"That's how you see yourself. I see myself being here. You can't go away because of your mother and Tony, and you figure that's killing your real life. People taking dope, they letting the dope kill their real lives 'cause they ain't strong enough to deal with it."

"What kind of real life you have around here, Motown?" Didi asked. "I mean, I'm not trying to put you down or anything, but you aren't living a big-time life, baby."

"I didn't say big-time," Motown said. "I just said real. What I do, I be doing it for real. I didn't even say it was good all the time."

"I can't buy that," Didi said. "What you have in life might be real, and what you're doing might be real, but isn't what you *want* something else? What do you *want* from life?"

"Nice people to be around, mostly," Motown said.

"Around here?"

"Maybe," Motown said, his dark face broadening into a smile. "If I tell them they make some good hamburgers, they'll stay around."

"Next time I get depressed I'll take my hamburger some-place else," Didi said, smiling.

"You have a boyfriend?" Motown asked.

"Not particularly," Didi said. "You have a girlfriend?"

"I don't think I've ever had a girlfriend," Motown answered.

"Which means what?" Didi asked.

"Don't mean nothing," Motown said.

"Then what you smiling at me for?"

"What you smiling at me for?"

"I'm not smiling at you," Didi said. "I'm just smiling because of what you said about the hamburgers."

"I'm just smiling because I'm happy you here," Motown said.

"That's a nice thing to say," Didi said. "It really is."

Motown stood and walked over to where Didi was just starting to put one of the hamburgers on a bun. He lifted her hand and kissed it. She looked at him, surprised, smil-ing. She leaned forward slightly, lifting her face toward his, and closed her eyes when he kissed her again.

CHAPTER VII

TALKING TO MOTOWN WAS ONE THING. FEELING GRATEFUL to him for having helped her was another. Even helping to set up the small apartment for him was done from a distance. She had told herself that it was interesting, a fun thing to do. But standing in front of him, her body pressed against his, the flat of his hand gentle against her cheek, his lips pressed tight against hers, was something else. No, she told herself, it shouldn't happen. But her heart was beating faster, and now her hands dug into his shoulders. One of his hands slid around her waist and pulled her even tighter against the firmness of his body. Their faces parted for an instant, and it was Didi who put her hand behind his head and pulled his mouth against her own again, who pushed herself into him until he nearly stumbled backwards.

"No!" Suddenly she pushed herself away. "No!"

She turned away from him, looking for her things. The room seemed smaller than it had ever been, pressing in on her, suffocating her. She grabbed her house keys and her change purse and almost staggered to the door.

"Didi?" His voice was gentle behind her, but she didn't stop, couldn't stop.

She ran down the stairs and into the hot, sultry evening. All the way home she could still feel the way his lips had felt on hers. The imprint of his body stayed on hers even as she walked down the street.

The streets—the streets were different. The colors ran from person to person. Black ran into brown and into beige and into yellow and almost white. Colors hipping and dipping, colors lean and clean in the hot Harlem afternoon, colors as she had never seen them before. What were they wearing? Red and green and yellow—they knew how to strut some color! Was it a celebration? A festival? The buildings sassed their angles, overlapping their lines with those of streetlamps and bus-stop shelters. Was this what it was like to be high? Was this the way the junkies felt, confused, dazed, hardly able to walk through streets as familiar as their own rooms?

Think, that's what Didi had to do. She had to think. You could fool the heart, but you couldn't fool the head. Now, what had happened? She would go over each incident, each movement, and see exactly why it had happened.

First, she had gone to his house to make dinner for him. It was a nice thing to do. She thought that he would like it. She had also thought about not seeing him again, but then she wanted to know if he would be all right in the place. She had liked the place, too, the way she had fixed it up for him.

Think about it carefully, she told herself. Yes, that's what had happened. She had cared for what he had done, and for the place, and what she herself had done for the place. Hadn't she taken a set of draperies, put one pair at the window and sewed the others together to make a covering for the pull-out cot? She had made the small apartment something special. That's what she cared for. Oh, yes, and she had kissed him lightly on the cheek, kissed him playfully, the way friends do. Then he had intruded himself, misunderstood what she was about and intruded himself. He had come to where she was standing and lifted her face to his and kissed her. He had put his lips against hers and made her feel—

No, I mustn't think about it, she said to herself. It was over. She wouldn't go back. She would write him a note, perhaps. She would say how sorry she was that he had misinterpreted her actions.

"Dear Mr. Williams," it would begin. "I am quite sorry that you did not understand my actions of the other day and took it upon yourself to kiss me. It means, of course, that you will never be able to see me again. Yours truly, Didi Johnson."

"You want something to eat?" Her mother was up and about. "I made some fish."

"No," Didi said, surprised that her mother was up, wanting to ask her how she was feeling but wanting even more to be alone.

"I'm sorry about being sick, honey." Didi's mother put a thin hand on her daughter's arm. "I'm really sorry."

"It's okay, Mama," Didi said. "Something will work out. Don't you worry about it."

Tony came home then. He had found a job in Brooklyn. Didi saw how tired he looked. He didn't look good.

"Mama seems to be feeling a little better," she said, searching for something to say.

"Yeah, that's good," Tony said. There was alcohol on his breath.

"How did the job go?"

"Okay, I guess." Tony turned away.

"There's some fish in the kitchen, if you're hungry."

"I got to go out," Tony said. "I'll grab a burger or something."

"You okay?"

"Yeah."

Just "yeah." No "mind your business," no anger that his big sister was showing concern for him. Didi felt Tony was still in trouble. But at least he was drinking and not using dope. At least she didn't see him using the dope.

She had heard of clinics where they kept people for months until they were drug-free. Maybe she would talk to Tony about going to one. They hadn't been close in years, but he knew that she cared for him. Even with all of his smart mouth, he had to know that. If he was in enough trouble, he might even listen to her.

It was what she didn't want. She didn't want to have to be around drug problems. She wanted to be around someone who thought about being a doctor, and about taking hansom cab rides around Central Park.

When she heard the door close behind Tony, she went in and checked on her mother. She was asleep. Didi pushed the hair away from her mother's face and straightened out the light bedspread.

She watched some television—there was a story on the news about a hit-and-run driver on the Lower East Side. Someone had hit a Cuban girl. She watched the reporter talk to the people of the neighborhood, worried mothers wondering why the police didn't do anything to stop the drag races in their neighborhood. Then she sat up quickly. There was someone in the background she thought she recognized. She watched the interviews carefully. The cameras panned the crowd again. The reporter's voice was over a picture of young people waving into the camera. "This is the third child to be hit by a speeding car . . ."

The face she thought she recognized was on the screen again. No, it wasn't Motown. It was someone less handsome, someone whose head wasn't held quite so high, whose shoulders did not sit so squarely over a well-muscled belly.

Didi went to bed, telling herself not to dream.

When she woke the next morning, she knew that she didn't have to think about Motown anymore. Her decision was made. She just wouldn't see him anymore. The boy definitely lacked understanding. And even if he didn't, she didn't want any more to do with him than she had to. She thought of calling up Bob Napier, a boy she had dated once or twice who had been accepted by the University of Pennsylvania. He was into coin collecting and classical music, but mostly coins. Maybe she would spend part of the summer with him. He had always liked her.

The next day her mother woke up more tired than usual. Didi realized that when she saw her mother up and about the day before, she had immediately jumped into hoping that her mother was miraculously recovered and that Didi would be able, after all, to go away to college.

"How you feeling this morning?" Didi asked.

"A little tired," her mother answered. "I got a pain in my arm."

"Which arm?" Didi asked, remembering that a pain in the left arm sometimes meant that a heart attack was starting.

"My left arm," her mother said. "I banged it into the closet door, and my elbow hurts something terrible. My own fault, though—I was the one left the door open."

"You put anything on it?" Didi asked, relieved that it was only a bruise.

"I was fixing to when you come home," her mother said. "But you seemed so upset and everything. I hate to see you like that, Didi, I really do."

"It wasn't anything, Mama," Didi said. "Just some fool kissed me. You want some coffee?"

"On the street?" Her mother's voice rose in alarm. "Did he touch you?"

"No." Didi couldn't help smiling. "In his apartment. I was . . . helping him get it together, but I didn't expect him to kiss me."

"It's somebody you know, then?" her mother asked.

"I know him." Didi rinsed the coffee pot out even though it was clean. "He's nice enough, I guess."

"What did you do when he kissed you?" her mother asked, her voice more relaxed now. "You kiss him back?"

"I suppose so," Didi said. "But that's all over now. I don't like him in that way. He did me a favor on the street once, and I was just returning it. I guess he thought it meant more than it did."

"Men are like that," Darlene said. "That's why you so

upset when you got home? I thought it was something else."

Didi carefully measured the coffee into the basket, put the top on the pot, and put it on the stove.

"The coffee will be ready in a while," Didi said. "If you want to lie down, I'll bring it in to you."

"No," Darlene said, "I'll stay up. I can't get my strength back in the bed. What's he look like, this boy?"

"Ugly," Didi said, smiling to herself.

It felt funny. She wanted to talk about him, to tell her mother about this guy who had had the nerve to just kiss her as if she were there to be kissed. Who didn't have one thing she wanted in a boyfriend.

"How ugly is he?" her mother asked.

"You think I like him," Didi asked, "don't you?"

"It's nice to have boys like you, whether you like them or not," her mother said.

That was it. It was nice having Motown like her, even though she didn't particularly care anything for him. It explained how she felt, kind of tingly inside, kind of nervous when she thought about him.

"I just don't want him to think that he has a chance to be anything more than a friend," Didi said. "You never can tell how they'll act sometimes."

"Especially when they're ugly," her mother said.

"He's not really that ugly," Didi said.

"I didn't think he'd be."

They had coffee and cinnamon toast and her mother asked her questions about Tony. She said that she had found an empty bottle of liquor in the closet in his room.

Maybe she was wrong about him using "other stuff."

Didi said that she also thought he wasn't using it anymore. The truth was that she didn't know and didn't want to know, until Tony reached the point where he would talk to her or would go for help. It would be ironic, she thought, if after all her dreams of getting away from the neighborhood, it was Tony who got away, if only to a drug rehabilitation center.

Didi thought about getting another job. She had put her name in with the school's vocational counselor, but nothing had shown up except some jobs at a fast-food restaurant. After the first week or so of vacation, she spent more time thinking about her school situation than a job. If she did have to stay in the city, she would have to work as well.

Her mother went back to bed and was soon asleep. Didi went and bought the *Times* and came back home to look through the want ads. Most of the jobs listings were with agencies; the few that weren't were mostly for secretaries or technical jobs. There was one for an editorial assistant with a book publishing firm. It asked for someone who was "a book lover and quick to learn." She called the number in the ad and spoke to a woman who apologized profusely that the ad hadn't mentioned that she would need to be a college graduate.

She had only applied to one local college and that was City University. She told herself at the time that City would be only a last resort—it wouldn't be any different from high school. She would still be living in the same place, still involved with the same kind of life. But would it be better if she didn't go to college at all?

She found the papers from City and called the Registrar's office.

Why had she waited so long? Didn't she realize that there was a great deal of competition to get into City University? Did she have a copy of her transcript? There was still a chance for her to get in on a matriculated basis if she came right down and completed the application forms. Of course, she could enter as a nonmatriculated student and still get credit for the courses once she did matriculate, but then she wouldn't be eligible for financial aid.

Didi changed into a powder-blue skirt and a yellow blouse with blue trim, then spent fifteen minutes looking for a blue belt before deciding to go with a wide, shiny black belt that she had bought at Macy's. Then she went down to City.

When she got home it was nearly five. She made ham patties, rice, and green peas for herself and her mother, cooking the ham patties in some pork gravy that came in a can.

Darlene picked at the food but said that she was feeling fine. She said that she had eaten some blueberry pie that Tony had brought her. Tony was asleep in his room. When Didi went into it she could smell the alcohol. There was a bottle of rye near the side of the bed. Tony had never been a drinker, and she was surprised that he had gotten into it so heavily.

She washed the dishes and then found a deck of cards to play gin with her mother, but Darlene had gone back to sleep. Didi turned on the television, twisting the dial and not finding anything she really wanted to watch, then settling for *Believe It or Not.* They had just started a story about someplace in India that considered rats to be sacred, when the doorbell rang.

"Motown, what are you doing here?" Didi said, trying to appear annoyed.

"Thought I'd come over and see if you was still mad," he answered.

"Not mad," Didi said. "In fact, I didn't even think about it at all after I left."

"Can I come in?" he asked.

"No," Didi said. "I don't think it's a good idea. If you want to go for a walk or something . . ."

Maybe if they had talked it would have been different. Didi could have explained to the boy how she just didn't feel anything for him and that he ought to know it so he wouldn't get hurt. She could have explained that she wasn't really sorry that they had kissed, but she was sorry that it didn't mean anything more than just a weird thing to do on a hot afternoon.

But they didn't talk as they walked, all the way to Riverside Drive. He didn't say a word, quiet as he was so often, and she didn't say anything either, not wanting to hurt him if he thought of their kissing the same way that she did—although she felt it probably meant a lot more to him than it did to her. Why else would he have come knocking on her door?

"What did you want to talk about?" she asked.

"Nothing," he said.

"Then why did you come all the way down to my house?" Didi stopped near a park bench.

"I was thinking about you," he said. "And when I think about you it makes me feel good. It does. So I was feeling good and I came over to see you."

"That doesn't make any sense," Didi said. They started walking again and their arms barely touched. Didi thought she should consider jogging or something. They hadn't walked that far but still she had difficulty breathing. She looked at Motown and he looked back at her and smiled. She couldn't let him think that walking with him meant anything.

"Look, Motown, there's something I have to get straight between us," Didi said. "That . . . you know . . . what happened at your place didn't mean anything, and I think we should make sure that it doesn't happen again. At least I want you to understand that it didn't mean anything from where I stand."

They were in the park and Motown turned and walked away from Didi. She watched him walk across the grass slowly. A young girl in a jogger's suit sat on a bench with headphones on. An old man, the white hairs on his bare chest gleaming in the late afternoon sun, played a flute, a towel spread before him. Motown walked over to a spot of shade under an elm tree and sat down.

Didi watched him as he looked out over the water, facing away from her. Then she turned and walked away. She walked slowly, wondering if he would follow, stopping now and then to watch one of the small children who'd been brought to the park by their mothers. Didi saw a black girl with a small white baby. The baby was playing in the dirt near the girl's feet while she read. Didi wondered how much the girl was getting paid to care for the child. She turned back to where Motown was still sitting.

When Motown had walked away from her without saying a word, she felt sorry at first, thinking that she had hurt him. But now it was Didi who felt hurt. It was Motown who had simply walked away, leaving her where she had said she wanted to be, without him.

She turned sharply, her full lips pursed with annoyance. She went back to where he sat and stood over him. He turned and looked up at her, raising one hand to shield his eyes.

"Well, how do you feel?" she asked. "I mean, you don't even know me that well so it couldn't be any big thing to you, either!"

Motown smiled.

"Smiling is not an answer," Didi said.

"Why don't you sit down?" Motown asked.

Didi sat far enough away from him so he wouldn't have any trouble getting the idea that she was annoyed.

"I'm sitting," she said. "And I see you're still smiling. Is something funny?"

Motown picked up a tuft of grass and rubbed it against his palm until the dirt fell loose. "If I had something good to say, I'd say it, but I don't. If I had some cool words I'd use them. I know you don't feel nothing, 'cause you keep saying it. But I know how I feel when I think about you."

"How do you feel?" Didi asked, knowing that she shouldn't.

"Like I just found out something wonderful," Motown said.

Didi didn't respond. She looked away and saw that the old man playing the flute had been joined by a woman. The woman looked younger than the man, perhaps ten years younger, but they were both probably past sixty, Didi thought. She looked over at Motown. A soft light filtered through the haze off the water. He would have looked better if he had on a better shirt. He was wearing a soft shirt without a collar. He would look nice, she thought, in a collar.

"So what did you find out?" Didi asked.

"How nice it is to be with you," he said.

"Yeah, well, you shouldn't have kissed me," she said.

"I know." Motown looked at her. He wasn't smiling. There was a calmness about him, an easy composure. "I'm glad I did, though."

"I shouldn't have kissed you back, either," Didi said. She smiled as she looked across the few feet that separated her from this boy. In the distance, the sun was fading, just a trace of its roundness still visible over the horizon. She wondered how she would manage the distance between them. Deciding that how didn't matter, she moved close to him.

At first he thought she was just getting ready to leave. Even when she drew very near him he wasn't sure. She put her hand on his chest, spreading her fingers and kissing him between her thumb and her forefinger. Then she lifted both of her hands and softly, so that her fingertips were scarcely tracing the muscles of his chest, brought them down to his waist and then around his back as far as she could reach and held tightly, so that she clung to him, almost as if she were afraid to let go, almost as if she were afraid to be holding him so.

He kissed her softly, slowly. She brought her face to him and he kissed it. He kissed her neck and her shoulders. She whispered his name as if she enjoyed his lips against her body and then she pulled away from him for a moment and looked at him, as if seeing him for the first time.

"You okay?" he asked.

"Sweetness." Her full lips formed the word carefully. "Sweetness."

"Didi." He said her name, not knowing better words or a better sound.

"Kiss me."

He kissed her with great patience, the way a starving man would eat his first meal, pretending that he wasn't hungry. Didi, in turn, kissed him and held him and clutched at the strong arms that did not know what to do with her softness and her eagerness for him, all the while telling herself that it couldn't be this way.

Motown didn't know how long they kissed or, after the kissing had stopped, how long they simply sat and held each other. But when they stopped it had grown cool, and the shadows were gathering quickly. Didi got up from where they were sitting, smoothed her skirt, and leaned weakly against the tree. Motown stood by her, taking wisps of grass from her hair. She came up to his shoulder as she

117:

looked up at him. The chain she was wearing was outside of her blouse, and he put it in again. She stood while he adjusted the top of her blouse.

"Motown, I don't want you to walk me home," she said. "I think I need to be alone."

"You want to drop by a friend of mine's place?" Motown asked. "Just for a minute?"

"Okay," she answered, curious about what kinds of friends Motown would have.

There were some people in The Spirit of Life bookshop when Motown and Didi arrived. They were interviewing the Professor for a piece on Harlem bookstores. Motown and Didi looked through some of the titles on the shelves until the Professor could get away.

"They are insisting that they take me to dinner," the Professor said.

"I just dropped by to say hello," Motown said.

"And the charming young lady?" The Professor smiled.

"A friend," Motown said, trying to cut off the grin that came across his face.

"How do you do, Motown's friend."

"Didi," she said, "my name's Didi Johnson."

"Motown, I have to go with these people," the Professor said. "If there's anything in the shop the young lady would like, you must give it to her for me."

"It's late," Didi said. "I have to get home."

"Perhaps another time?"

Didi nodded.

Outside, Motown was still smiling. He was glad that the Professor had seen Didi.

"You're full of surprises," Didi said. "Nice ones."

"Can I come to see you tomorrow?" he asked. "If you're not busy, I mean?"

"No, call me," she said. "Let me see how I feel first. Okay?"

"Sure."

He walked her to St. Nicholas Avenue and she squeezed his hand quickly and started home alone. Motown, so filled with the moment that he could hardly see what was going on around him, stopped for a hamburger and Coke, ate them with relish, and then walked home slowly, reliving his moments with Didi over and over again.

Tutmose Rogers lived with his parents just off Lenox Avenue. His father had worked as a school janitor until he retired in 1962, the year in which Tutmose was born. Some said it was because his father was so old when he was born and didn't really have the energy or inclination to play with him much that Tutmose was slow. Others said that Tutmose wasn't really slow at all; it was just that he was an old man's child and therefore serious by nature. Whatever the case, Motown had always liked Tutmose, and for the three years that the two young men had known each other, they had made a practice of going out to dinner together at least once a month. Sometimes they went to McDonald's; other times they went to Ruby's or to the Chinese restaurant on 125th near Broadway. Motown didn't mind that Tutmose was a little slow, because most people just talked about foolishness anyway.

"Where you want to go?" Tutmose asked, picking up

any trash that was lying around the newsstand that his father had bought for him two years before.

"Let's go to the Chinese place," Motown said, knowing that The Jade Palace was his friend's favorite.

"That's okay with me," Tutmose said.

"You know what we're going to do next time?" Motown took the sunshade down from the green kiosk and handed it to Tutmose. "The next time we're going to eat at my place. I can't cook much but I can cook a little."

"I don't know if I'll like that," Tutmose said. The most enjoyable part of having dinner out was letting people see that he had a friend and was doing the same things that what he called "regular" people were doing. In a way, Motown wasn't a "regular" person to Tutmose, because he had lived in abandoned buildings most of the time Tutmose had known him. The fact that they were both, in their own ways, different from others created a bond between them.

"Well, maybe not when we eat out," Motown said. "But sometime you're going to have to come up and see the place I have."

"Yo!" It was Carlos, one of Touchy's boys. "Motown, what you doing away from the telephone booth, man?"

"What you mean?" Motown asked.

"I thought that you stayed near a telephone booth all the time," Carlos said. He had an ivory toothpick that dangled from the corner of his mouth. "That way anytime anything went down you didn't like, you could hop on into that telephone booth and make like you Superman."

"He ain't got time for you to be talking no foolishness,"

Tutmose said. "We going to get us something to eat."

"You seen Reggie around?" Carlos was thin, and his skin was an even brown color, which seemed to complement the soft pink shirt and tan slacks he wore.

"I ain't looking for him," Motown said.

"He looking for you, chump." Carlos started walking down to The Starlight. "You just stay here—I'll see if he's in the club."

"C'mon, let's go," Tutmose said. "They don't mean nothing but some trouble, that's all."

"They don't bother me," Motown said. "We got plenty of time."

Tutmose looked around the kiosk until he found the lock, made sure that he had his keys, and then locked up. He told Motown he was ready to go, but Motown wouldn't go right away.

"All you young men are warriors," the Professor had said. "You walk these streets testing your manhood, seeing who is the best. And the bad thing is you're afraid to back down because you're boxed in. The tenements box you in, the fire escapes make cages for you. But you're fighting for what you should be sharing. These Harlem streets belong to all of us. You earned your share when you were born black. That's when you earned your share. When we going to learn that? When we going to learn it?"

"You know, if you back down, people gonna say you a punk," Motown had said, knowing it wasn't what the Professor wanted to hear.

"A punk? You don't see white men out in the streets fighting and killing their own, do you?" the Professor had asked. "That's not how they prove their manhood. They prove theirs in the stock market, on the job, in politics."

"If you can't be no man the way they do it," Motown said, "you got to be one the best way you can."

Carlos came out of The Starlight first, then Lavelle, Touchy, and Reggie. Touchy walked across the street and got into his car. Lavelle and Carlos stopped about twenty feet from where Motown and Tutmose were standing, and Reggie, his head to one side, came up to them.

"Hey, sucker, what you doing around here?" Reggie spat on the sidewalk between himself and Motown. He was wearing a light green jacket, slacks, and a pair of scuffed wingtip shoes.

"What do you want?" Motown asked.

"What do I want?" Reggie grinned. "Last time I saw you on One-Two-Five Street you was talking your big talk. Now you sounding like a lame. How come you ain't running down that line about if I want you all I got to do is leap on over and get you? Don't tell me you feeling a little punkified today?"

Reggie was acting cool, too cool. There was no way that he could take Motown by himself. Motown figured either Lavelle and Carlos were going to get into it or else Reggie was carrying.

"You got a problem?" Motown asked.

"C'mon," Tutmose said, "let's go get some Chinese food."

"I heard you had a problem," Reggie said, "getting into everybody's business and everything."

"Who told you that?" Motown asked.

"I think it was your mama," Reggie said.

"Got no respect for each other, got no love for each other," the Professor had said. "But what can you expect when you don't even know who you are? You don't know what kind of a people you from? You got to be able to respect yourself before you can respect anybody else."

"Why don't we make this another day?" Motown said. "I really don't have time for no mess today."

He turned and started walking away quickly, hoping that he hadn't guessed wrong. Reggie would need more time to intimidate him if he was going to try anything alone, even if he were carrying. He would need to say something else, to prolong the confrontation.

"Where you going, punk?"

"C'mon, Tutmose," Motown called over his shoulder. "Let's go get some Chinese food."

Motown walked quickly, away from the direction of Lavelle and Carlos. He could sense, could feel Reggie coming after him. He waited until Reggie had almost reached him, then turned around. Over Reggie's shoulder he could see that neither Lavelle nor Carlos had moved. Reggie had to be carrying.

"I got something—'

Reggie never finished the sentence. Motown stepped into him and hit him with everything he had about six inches below the belt. Reggie doubled over and Motown pushed him all the way to the ground. Then he dropped on him, the weight of his body following his knee into the small of Reggie's back. There was a loud grunt, and Motown saw both of Reggie's hands on the pavement. He quickly twisted him over, then opened his jacket.

The pistol didn't look to be more than the kind that kids played with in the street. It was dark gray, with black electrician's tape around the handle. Motown held it in his hand, looked around until he saw an empty sewer drain, and then went over and dropped it in.

On the ground Reggie writhed in pain.

"C'mon, Tutmose." Motown started for the Chinese restaurant with his friend.

"You a bad dude," Tutmose said in the restaurant. "You tore that cat up!"

Motown nodded and braced the menu against the table so that his hands wouldn't shake. He felt a growing wave of nausea. There was pain in his side, and in the pit of his stomach, and now in the front of his head. He hadn't remembered being hit, he knew he hadn't been, but all the same, he hurt badly. He thought of what Didi had said about not wanting to have to deal with these things, these people. For a moment he tried to focus on what Tutmose was saying; then he took a deep breath and collapsed across the table.

"Hey, Didi, wake up!" Tony shook his sister by the elbow until she stirred.

" 'Way!"

"What?"

"Go away!"

"Look, I got to talk to you," Tony said. "It's important."

Didi felt to make sure that her pajama top was reasonably closed, then sat up in bed. She blinked her eyes open briefly, noted that it was morning, then fell back across the pillow.

"Talk," she mumbled from beneath a sheet that should have been changed two days before.

"You ever see that dude—what's his name?" Tony snapped his fingers twice, trying to jog his memory. "Oh, yeah, Motown."

"Yeah, I've seen him," Didi said. "So what."

"I been thinking about him," Tony said. "I guess he's an all-right guy. You know, he don't look square, but I guess he is."

"Go on." Didi sat up.

"I been thinking about a lot of things," Tony said. "I think maybe I can't handle what I'm into. You know what I mean?"

"No, not exactly," Didi said. "I see you've been drinking a lot."

"That little chippy I had, using stuff on the weekends and things, well, it's grown up now," Tony said. "I keep telling myself about how I'm going to be cutting back and stuff, but it ain't working out like I thought it would."

"It's getting worse?"

"I don't know if it's getting any worse, but I know it sure ain't getting no better." Tony had on a pair of dark slacks that were shiny from wear and a soft yellow shirt.

He was a good-looking guy, as his mother said. He reminded Didi of pictures she had seen of her father when he was young.

"I guess you don't want to tell me about it?" Didi asked.

"You mind listening?"

"No." She pulled her knees up to her chin and put her arms around her legs.

"At first Touchy was letting me have a little action on the weekends. He said it was cool for his product for people to see me nice on the weekend without being wrecked all week."

"That's how you built up the chippy?"

"Yeah, but it wasn't no chippy," Tony said. "You want me to make some tea or something? There some instant coffee in the closet?"

"Is the water on?"

"No."

"Don't bother—why don't you go on."

"The more I looked around, the more I seen that the bread I was making from Touchy I was giving it right back under the table. I was getting some of the stuff free from Touchy, but I was buying the rest of it downtown so that people wouldn't know how much was using. I didn't even want to think about that shit myself, really."

"Did you really think it was something that you wanted to do with your life?"

"No, not the dope part, but the other part," Tony said. He stood and went to the window. There was the sound of a fire engine passing on the street below. "You know, I was blowing all them things I used to want. 'Member when we used to stay home sometime and talk about what we were going to do?"

"I was going to be the first woman president and you were going to be the top general of my army."

"Yeah." Tony smiled. "Yeah, that kind of thing. We had some dreams and stuff, and it all seemed cool, but it was just getting away from me. What really set it off was when everybody in school was talking about applying for college later and stuff. I was jacking off in high school and I knew I'd have to pull some kind of miracle to get into college and another one to make it if I did get in, see? Then I thought that maybe I'd just go out and find a job and say 'later' for it. But, you know, you think about a job doing something cool. I went down to a few agencies and told them I had finished high school. They bought that all right, but they didn't even send me out on nothing but some messenger jobs. The best thing they offered me was what they called an inventory clerk. I was supposed to go around to supermarkets on weekends and count groceries. That was just when they needed me."

"It would've been better than the dope," Didi said. She put her arm on Tony's shoulder.

"No, it wouldn't," Tony said, his head down. "Anything I blew with the dope was the dope's fault. It wasn't me that was just naturally messed up."

"How can you say that?" Didi's eyes had filled with tears. "Don't say that. You're not messed up, naturally or any other way."

"Then why am I sitting here like this?" Tony asked. "Sitting here puking my guts out to you. You know this ain't like me. I'm messed up and I need some help."

"The thing you got to do is to kick the habit," Didi said.

"No, the thing I got to do is to want to kick the habit," Tony said. "I know all the ways to kick the thing—I just ain't doing it. And if I get it cut back, I just start going back to it again."

"Oh, my God!" Didi put her head on Tony's shoulder and let the tears flow easily from her. Her body shook with sobs, and she clenched her teeth so the sound wouldn't wake their mother.

"I've been trying to cut back with liquor," Tony said, disengaging himself. "Every time I needed to get high, I'd try to get drunk instead, but it don't work."

"You could go away to one of those clinics," Didi said. "They have special places for people with drug problems. I've read about them in the papers."

"Yeah, I know about them. They ain't that easy to get into. This Puerto Rican social worker told me that the real good ones cost a lot of money. The others have a waiting list about yea long. I thought maybe if you could come down to the place with me I could fill out the papers, and them seeing you, they'd know ı was serious and stuff."

"And you are serious?"

"If you knew what my life is like you'd know that cancer ain't no more serious than I'm being now."

"Then we have to do something about it," Didi said, softening her tone. "You know, Tony, I'm really in your corner. Even though it sounds like I'm coming down on you a little hard sometimes. In a funny way, even though he doesn't really know you, Motown is in your corner, too."

"Yeah, hey, right." Tony snapped out of himself for the moment. "Look, he was all right, and that's why I wanted to tell you that there's a contract out on him."

"A what?"

"The people downtown was saying that Touchy couldn't handle his territory," Tony said. "After what happened with you going to the Man and then him trying to set me up."

"Trying to set you up?" Didi looked at him. "What do you mean?"

"He set me up to get busted," Tony said. "That was supposed to teach you a lesson, I guess. Anyway, Motown was the one that messed both things up. That's why Touchy really means business. Reggie was supposed to shoot him, but Motown took his gun yesterday. Now everybody saying that he took Reggie off the case and put somebody else on. The way I figure it, it got to be Carlos. I heard Carlos got ten big bills and some change for wasting a cat once before."

"I know where he lives," Didi said. "I'll go warn him. Does anyone else know where he lives?"

"No, but they don't figure they have to with Motown," Tony said. "You know he don't back down from nothing."

"Look, can we go down to see about the clinic tomorrow?" Didi had reached her closet and was looking for something to wear.

"Not until the day after tomorrow," Tony said. "That's when the lady comes around—you know, the social worker."

CHAPTER VIII

CHICAGO—DIDI THOUGHT ABOUT MOTOWN GOING TO Chicago. There were lots of black people there, and she was sure they wouldn't follow him. He didn't have that much, and everything he did have was old, except for a few shirts. She would write to him. He would answer but he wouldn't put his return address on the envelope. Later, perhaps even years later, they would see each other somewhere and have cocktails and wonder how they had ever made it out of the ghetto. She stopped twice on the way to make sure that she wasn't being followed. She had even thought badly of Tony—perhaps it was just a trick of his to find out Motown's address. No, Tony was hurt. He was hurt and depressed and feeling about as low as she had ever seen him. This wasn't the same Tony who had told her to mind her own business just a few short weeks ago. This was someone different, a stranger who had moved into the flesh of her brother and had eaten out his insides.

Later she would go and see the social worker about Tony. First she would go to Motown and tell him what Tony had said. Perhaps he could go to the West Side Highway and start hitchhiking out of town. She would go with him and stand by the road and kiss him as the car that would take him out of her life slowed down to pick him up.

The sun was brilliant, the day already too hot. She was perspiring under her arms; the long-sleeved top had been a bad choice. No matter. She rang his bell, and a long minute later he opened the front door.

"Come up with me, quick!" Didi rushed past Motown into the dim hallway. She started quickly up the winding stairway, glancing back just once to make sure that he was fast on her heels, and was out of breath by the time they reached his door.

"You've got to get your stuff packed up in a hurry and get out of here." Didi was gasping for breath. "Tony just told me that Touchy put out a contract on you. That means they're going to hire someone to kill you."

"Yeah, Reggie came up to me yesterday with a gun," Motown said. "I ain't going nowhere. Where I'm gonna go?"

"Where you're going to go? What difference does it make? If you don't go somewhere you're going to be killed!"

Motown shrugged and went to the small refrigerator. He opened it and took out some orange juice and poured out two glasses as Didi stared at him.

"Motown, do you understand what I'm saying to you?"

"I understand what you saying," Motown said. "You saying that Touchy supposed to be trying to get somebody to kill me, right?"

"Tony thinks that he's going to get Carlos to do it," Didi said. She stood directly in front of Motown so he could see her face. "And if he doesn't get Carlos, all he has to do is to get some of those junkies—they'd kill their own mothers for a fix."

"Yeah, but I ain't going no place," Motown said. "I didn't do nothing. I ain't got no place to run to, or no place to hide in. What I'm going to do, go sit in some hole and give up my living 'cause of Touchy? Might as well be dead one way as another."

"You're just going to wait here until some one of his junkie friends finds out where you live and then comes and kills you? You don't have anything here. A little while ago you were sleeping in abandoned buildings. You told me you don't like your job. What are you staying here for?"

"Maybe nothing," Motown said. "Maybe that's the way I am."

"A fool?"

He looked at her. Looked to see who she was, what face she could wear when she told him that he didn't have anything here. He didn't recognize her, though. She was someone else, a girl standing in his doorway trying not to look at the cracked plaster walls and the old mattress he slept on.

She kept on talking but he wouldn't listen. He shut her out of his mind and thought about what he would have for dinner that night.

"Don't you understand that these people are serious?" Didi was pleading with him with her hands. "They really intend to kill you!"

Maybe he would buy some hamburger and some buns and make hamburgers. He didn't buy many hamburgers from stands, but he liked them. He could go to McDonald's and get two orders of french fries and put them into the oven until the burgers were done.

"I think that the only reason that Tony even told me was because he felt guilty. In his heart he has to be grateful to you for what you did. Did you know that he was being set up by Touchy? That's the kind of people you're dealing with. Not reasonable people."

He wanted her to leave. For the first time since they had met, in their very little knowing of each other, he wanted her to go away. He realized that what he had been telling himself, that he thought she was too good for him, that he would never be able to really have her to love, was a lie. He did think that he would have her to love; he was hoping with all of his heart and all of his being that he would have her to love.

Didi went on with her reasons why he should leave.

There had been times when he was in a foster home and something would happen—some small gesture, some word, a smile—and hope that he would finally have a home would flicker across his mind like the shadow of a bird, gone almost before he knew it. He would force it away from him. When he was seven he used to dig his fingernails into the palms of his hands whenever the woman he was staying with made him sit on her lap.

Didi went on with her reasons why he should leave.

Once he was walking through the Port Authority building and a brown-skinned girl with a friendly smile and sparkling gray-green eyes had walked up to him and said that he looked like he needed a flower and could she give him one. He said yes, and she did. Then she asked him for a donation, and when he had given her a quarter that he needed more than sparkling gray-green eyes ever would, she turned her friendly smile away.

"Now *what* are you going to do?" Didi was saying.

"I'm not going away," Motown said. "Only thing I know are these streets and these people. That's not much, as I should know, but it's some. Only friends I got is you, Tutmose, and the Professor."

"Look, Motown," she said, hoping that he wouldn't look at her. "I enjoyed kissing you in the park but, I always enjoy kissing guys. You know what I mean?"

"Yeah." The word came low, from his chest.

"So if you're staying around because you're a friend of mine, you're not staying for a very good reason."

"That's the way it is," Motown said.

"I'm leaving now," she said. "And I think you should leave as soon as you can."

No answer.

She turned and walked away from him. She went through the door. She walked down the stairs stiff-legged, clutching the banister. What was it with this guy? In the park, now, in his apartment before. What was it that she was always walking away from him? Why were the steps so hard? She had come to him today to do him a good turn, to tell him that he was in danger and that he was being a fool. What was it with this guy? She didn't want to think about what was going to happen to him, even though she had lied about kissing other boys and she had lied about not being a friend of his. But that's where it ended. Friendship. She wasn't in love with him. No way. Not for a tiny little moment, she told herself, almost believing it. She was afraid for him and didn't know what to do. She cried as she left his place and spoke his name softly.

Sometimes in the early morning, between the sleepless night and daybreak, she thought of making love to him. She wondered what it would be like and thought of all the things that she had heard. It was not what she wanted— this love-making that faded by morning and left babies that would anchor even the smallest dreams. What had her mother said? "That sweatin' and gruntin' don't lead to nothin' but some more sweatin' and gruntin'." But still Didi thought about it, and in her mind it was more than sweating and grunting and making babies. It was thinking about his dark flesh tight against her own soft brown skin and kissing him and holding him. That's what it was about. That, a warmth in her stomach, and the way her thighs tingled when she stroked them softly and thought about him. But she wasn't in love with the dude. No way.

Most of the time Motown didn't hurt. He hadn't hurt in a long time. The parts were still there, deep inside, the parts that could be touched and send him screaming into his own dark shadows. They were still there. But he had reached out as he walked through the streets and had felt the hard power of the walls, the red brick and brownstone walls, the graffiti-scarred walls that lined each block and had made them a part of himself. He had learned to be almost untouchable, almost unfeeling. Almost.

But now he had opened a crack in the walls. He had opened himself to this girl, and the emotions flooded in

135:

around this tiny feeling he had allowed himself and filled his every sense.

He thought of Reggie. He hadn't been afraid at the time. He knew how to defend himself. He was good with his hands. He had the heart to do the part, as they said, so the starring role was his. But later, when he thought about it, sitting there in the restaurant with Tutmose, the heart left him.

He was tired, but not in the same way that Didi said that she was tired. Didi was tired of the streets and of the Reggies. Motown wasn't tired of the streets, he loved them. He wasn't even tired of Reggie. He knew Reggie. The dude wasn't much. He was weak. You could see his eyes darting around looking to see who was looking at him, afraid that someone would find him out. Even with the gun he was weak, flapping his lips to get his courage up. That's the way it was sometimes. Motown knew that. He had often looked around for something to lean on himself. Sometimes you needed that. And Motown knew about being tough. He had walked down the streets himself, a toothpick dangling from his mouth, daring anybody in the world to look him in the eye. And if they looked at him, he would shoot them back a glance that would curdle water, that would make a blind man blink, that would stop babies from growing. And when they looked away they wouldn't see that he was afraid, or alone.

He was making a delivery on Seventy-fifth Street. It was to a large apartment building with a doorman. The doorman, a squat, barrel-chested man, looked up from *El Diario* and then at the number of the apartment the clothes were going to. Motown knew that if there was a tip involved, the doorman would take the clothes up himself.

"Six B," the man said.

The inside hallway was cool and dim. A large plant stood near the elevator door. Motown watched the indicator light above the elevator until it reached "M" for Main.

What kinds of people lived in places like this? Motown wondered. He imagined that they would have lots of money. He couldn't imagine that you would have many problems if you had lots of money.

"Who's there?" The voice that came through the door was timid and cracking.

"I got your clothes from the cleaners," Motown said.

There was a clicking sound, a moment of silence, and then the door cracked open. Motown could see part of a face and thin white fingers on the edge of the door. The door closed and opened again.

"Come in," she said.

Motown brought the clothing in.

"There should be three dresses and one blouse," the woman said. She looked at them carefully as Motown held the hangers.

"Come with me. I have some other things for you to take."

"Yes, ma'am."

Motown followed her from the small foyer through a large, almost cheery living room into a bedroom. The bedroom was light, and the sun came through open venetian blinds and lace curtains. She took the clothes from Motown and laid them across the bed. Then she opened a closet by sliding away the door, revealing a long row of dresses.

"I don't get out too much," she said. "But I like to keep my things nice. It you keep them cleaned they stay nice."

"Yes, ma'am."

The dresses that he had brought from the cleaners looked like the kind that Motown had seen in old-fashioned pictures. The ones in the closet were the same.

"I'm Marie Van Ripper," she said. "My family is one of the oldest in the country."

"Yes, ma'am."

"I don't make a great deal of fuss about it because that's not the kind of person I am," Mrs. Van Ripper said. "Although if I start going out more I just might."

"Yes, ma'am."

"It doesn't hurt to remember who you are in this life," she went on. The thin white arm that selected a dress to be dry-cleaned had a fold of skin that hung from armpit to elbow. "Are you from an old family?"

"I'm from an old people," Motown said. "We go back to the beginning of time."

She stopped looking at the dress in the closet to turn to look at Motown. He was at least a foot taller than she was, and she had to look up at him. She didn't lift her chin, but kept it down and looked up at him sidewise with quick bird's-eye glances.

"You wouldn't know it just by looking at you," she said. "That's like me, you couldn't tell that I was somebody unless I wanted you to know it."

She selected two more dresses, gave them to Motown

on the hangers, and then sent him into the foyer while she went someplace in the large apartment and produced a quarter for him.

CHAPTER IX

"GREETINGS, PRINCESS." THE PROFESSOR TOOK DIDI'S HAND. "I'm pleased to see you here."

"Thanks," Didi said. "I wasn't sure whether this was your busy time or not . . ."

"Unfortunately I don't have enough busy times in this place. Someone has discovered that my people have a great oral tradition, and the fool who brought the message said that it meant we didn't know how to read," the Professor said. "So my busiest times are in the playground of my imagination, where I am always young enough to participate. When I'm lucky, I get someone as charming as you through the doors."

"Thanks," Didi said, smiling. "I just wondered if I could talk to you about something."

"Would you like tea?"

"Please."

"You're the young lady that came in with my young friend Motown, aren't you?" The Professor opened the top of the brass teapot, looked in, was satisfied with what he saw, and put it down again.

"That's right," Didi said. "I'm really worried about him.

You're the one person in the world he really seems to trust and listen to. I was surprised that he read so much."

"He's a good young man," the Professor said. He had placed a cup in front of Didi and filled it carefully with tea. "His heart is in the right place, but more importantly, his head is in the right place as well."

"Can I tell you just what's going on and what I want you to do?" Didi asked.

"By all means." The Professor smiled at her.

"My brother has been using dope and I found out about it," Didi said. "I thought the right thing to do would be to go to the police and get them to arrest the guy who's selling the stuff in the street. I did that, but it didn't do any good. The police just started asking me what kind of evidence I had, and that kind of thing. You know what I mean?"

"If nine-year-old addicts can find the people who are selling drugs, the police surely can," the Professor said.

"Right. So the guy who was selling the drugs, the one I told the police about, got some guys to beat me up. Motown was just coming along when he saw it and he stopped them. So then they've been mad at him ever since."

"He did this?"

"Right, and then, later, when Touchy tried to get my brother arrested, Motown stopped that, too."

"So now he's made quite an enemy of this Touchy person?"

"Right," Didi said. "And the word on the street is that Touchy has put out a contract—what I mean is, that Touchy wants to have Motown killed. I told Motown that he should leave, go someplace else where they can't get him, but I don't think he wants to listen to me."

"And what you thought I could do was to convince him to leave before he gets hurt."

"Yes," Didi said.

The Professor lifted the tea to his lips and sipped it slowly. A flood of thoughts came to him, tumbled in his mind, snatches of conversation, images of himself and Motown sitting at the same carved table where he and Didi now sat.

"Didi. What is this name from?" the Professor asked.

"My father thought it would be cute," Didi answered. "That's about it, I guess."

"Cute? I see." The Professor closed his eyes for a moment. "There was an Egyptian queen with a similar name, I just wondered. Well, Didi, the problem is, I'm not quite sure what you want me to do."

"Tell him to leave New York," Didi said. "At least leave Harlem."

"If a man walks down the street there could be many things that he is doing. He could be going to work. He could be exercising his limbs. Perhaps he is looking for some article he has lost. What will Motown be doing if he leaves?"

"Like what?"

"Do you want him to run off alone and hide from the world because he is afraid of what might happen? Do you want him to give up what he has here and look for it somewhere else? Do you want him to leave because if he came to harm it would embarrass you? You see, if I am to tell him to leave Harlem, then I'd have to tell him what he is to be doing. I would have to say, Motown, a young woman thinks it is too dangerous for you to live here, and rather than worry about you she would rather have you run away."

"I don't mean to be disrespectful, sir," Didi said. "But his life is in danger and philosophy isn't going to change that. And he doesn't have anything to stay here for in the first place."

"Then there's no danger," the Professor said. "If you have nothing to lose, there is no risk."

"Those are good-sounding words, but that's all," Didi said.

"Let me tell you something," the Professor said. "I don't want to see this boy hurt. I love him as if he was my own son. No, I love him more. I love him the way an old man loves his only son. When I am gone, all that will be left of me are the few books that I've given away—I don't sell that many—and a few wild thoughts that I have planted in that young man's mind. So when I speak like this to you it's not because I love the sound of my own voice, but because I just can't tell him to go away from me without giving him something of me to take with him."

"I like him, too," Didi said. "That's why I'm here. If I didn't like him I wouldn't have come."

The Professor made a gesture, as if he was going to speak and then stopped it in midair. He looked about him until he spotted an old fan on a shelf. He went to it and pushed the switch to the "on" position. Nothing happened for a while and then, slowly, the blades of the fan began to turn.

Pleased, the old man came back to the table.

"You come here," he said, "with youth filling your blouse and worry filling your face and you tell me that you have carefully added up the good points and the bad points of this young man and have come to the startling conclusion that, all things considered, you like him. Is that so?"

"Not the way you put it," Didi said.

"Then tell me, how would you put it? How would you put it? How would you put it if nothing else mattered in the world? If there were no one else's face to look into except this old black face of mine? How would you put it then?"

The fan turned slowly, ever so gently stirring the warm air without turning one paper, not even one of the yellowed flyers on the Professor's shelves. A minute passed slowly, using its moments to tilt the edges of reason.

"I love him," Didi said. And then, looking up at the Professor, into his once dark eyes now gray-veiled with age, her own brown eyes filled with tears of happiness for the thought that she did indeed love Motown.

"I love him," she said again.

"And he knows this?"

Didi shook her head. No, she hadn't told him that she loved him. But she would. She would tell him, and the thought of it made her feel gladder than anything had ever made her feel before.

"After you tell him," the Professor said, "I will see what I can do."

The brilliant sun of the late afternoon hurt her eyes as she left the Professor's small bookstore. She felt light-hearted and light-footed, wanting to run and dance down the streets and barely resisting the temptation to stop perfect strangers on the street and tell them the news. She saw other couples walking down the street and felt happy for them and wished that they knew about her and Motown so that they could share her joy.

Go to his house, she thought. Walk the streets so that there wouldn't be too long to wait. Smile at the people.

"Hey, Sister." A stringy dude in front of The Silver Rail leaned toward her, not wanting to relinquish his spot near the neon sign. "You sure looking good—somebody must be taking *good* care of you."

"That's right!" Didi answered.

"Walk on, mama!"

She walked on. She strutted on. Carrying it high for the world to see. She passed a funeral parlor down from Small's and saw that it was five-thirty. He might already be home.

Motown had thought of stopping at a resturant, but instead he decided to try his hand again at cooking and picked up a package of franks at the delicatessen. He was halfway home when he remembered that he had forgotten the rolls and was just starting back when he saw her. He turned to see Didi near his stoop. He was glad to see her, the way he was often glad to see things that pleased but did not particularly concern him. And what he had told himself was that he would not let Didi particularly concern him. He would go back, as the Professor had said, and as the old white woman had said as he stood, waiting for the quarter tip in her apartment, to "remembering who he was."

Still, he was glad to see her. He was, he knew, after all these years of living alone, reaching a point at which even those things that later caused disappointment were good. Would he ever forget holding Didi in the park? Would he ever forget kissing her? Or feeling her lips against his? How many times had he remembered her putting her tongue into his mouth and then being embarrassed about it?

"Hey, what's happening?" he said.

"Just getting in from work?"

"Yeah, picked up some franks from the store down the street but I forgot the rolls. You want to go with me to get some?"

"I came over to talk to you, really," Didi said. "You want to talk a while and then go out?"

"Okay."

"You're quiet," she said, taking his hand. "You mad about what I said yesterday?"

"No," he said. "I'm not hopping up and down, celebrating it, or nothing like that, though."

"You got to know where I'm coming from," Didi said. "Black women have to be careful about what they're doing. It shouldn't have to be a thing where you choose between liking someone or being something, but that's the way it seems sometimes. You know what I mean?"

"No."

"Yes, you do," Didi said. They had reached his door and he fished through his pockets for his keys.

They went in and up to his apartment again. She wondering if he was going to be difficult and he trying to picture how he had left the apartment in the morning.

"I could cook the franks," he said, when they had entered the apartment.

"You hungry?"

"A little."

"Okay." Didi sat at the card table that served as dining-room table, desk, and counter space for Motown. "What I mean is that so many young women find themselves married at eighteen, pregnant before they know it, and trapped on welfare or in some . . . some . . ."

"Some place like this?" Motown asked.

"Yeah," Didi said. "Someplace like this. I just don't want this."

"You told me that before," Motown said. "I know how you feel. I guess it all works out to what you want. You looking to get away from black people—"

"Not black people." Didi held her hand up to stop Motown. "What I want to do is to get away from some things that go on here. You know what I mean?"

"I never had that much choice I can start turning down people to like," Motown said.

"You want me to make those franks?" Didi asked, standing.

"No." Motown had thought of boiling the franks and then changed his mind. He put a large pat of margarine in the pan and watched as it melted.

"You wondering why I came," Didi said, "since I'm saying the same old thing?"

"I think you're wondering why you came, too," Motown said. He took the franks from the cellophane wrapping, rinsed them off in the sink, and put three in the pan. The water hitting the grease popped and he ducked away from it.

"I was telling myself that I didn't want to live in Harlem, and I didn't want to tie myself down to a life that I didn't want. What I wasn't saying to myself, or saying to you, or maybe even admitting to myself, is that I love you."

"Oh."

"Oh?" Didi looked at him. "That's it?"

"You don't like where I live—"

"I didn't say that, I just said that I wouldn't want to be trapped in a place like this forever," Didi said.

"What you saying is that you love me but I don't fit your program, right?"

Didi started crying. Motown stood in front of the stove looking at her, not knowing what to do. He was sorry for what he had said, perhaps sorrier than for anything he had ever said before. What would she do? Maybe she would just walk away, just leave. What he would have liked to do was to make it better, if just for that moment. He remembered once when he was with a family in Queens and the social worker from the county had come to pick him up he had made a paper airplane for the woman he had called Mama for almost six months. She had smiled and it had made him feel better to see her smile. Her standing there at the front door was the only picture he ever had of her in his mind.

"Didi," he searched for words. "I'm sorry."

"I'm sorry, too," she said. Her lips quivered and her

eyes still filled with tears as she clutched both sides of the chair. Motown stood there, scarcely breathing.

The franks sizzled in the pan. Motown turned them off and wiped his hands on a towel.

"Don't you know anything . . . anything wonderful to say?" Didi said, her voice cracking with emotion.

Motown went to where Didi was sitting and knelt before her so that he was looking into her face and could feel the warmth of her breath on his own face.

"I don't know nothing wonderful to say," he said, "but Didi, I do love you. I can't do nothing wonderful either but if I could I'd do it for you. If I could jump around and fly and stuff like that, I'd do it for you and so everybody could see I was doing it for you, too. I'd do anything for you."

"Then could you hold me for a while?"

On his knees before her, he put both arms around her and she put hers under his and clung to him. She pulled him tightly against her, moving her legs so that they were on either side of him, and around him and holding him as tightly as were her arms.

Then she began to kiss him and he kissed her back. He kissed her softly, his lips making small sounds as he did. Didi kissed Motown harder than he kissed her. She pulled him to her harder and let her fingers squeeze into his muscular arms.

"I love you, I love you, I love you." She said the words over and over again. Letting them rush from her lips between kisses.

"I love you too," Motown said, pulling his face from

hers. She looked at him, stood up before him, and pulled him to his feet. She put her arms under his shoulders and pulled their bodies together, digging her nails into his back as her breasts slid across his chest.

"We'd better get out of here," Didi said, pushing herself away from him. "I think I need some air."

He knew he loved her. In spite of what he had told himself about not really wanting to, he loved her. In a way it made him feel sad, knowing that he would be opening himself up to all of the moments of pain later on. With the foster mothers he had been able, in the last years of his being with them, to shut them away from his affection. But with Didi, there was no shutting away. She came at him as no one ever had before, filling his dreams and his waking moments as well. If there was to be pain later, it wouldn't be his fault, he told himself. What else could he do except love Didi Johnson?

CHAPTER X

OUTSIDE IT WAS STILL WARM BUT THE AIR WAS COOLER than it had been in the apartment. Didi clung to Motown's arm as they walked along. She was patting her hair into place with her free hand. She looked at Motown and smiled, and he could see that she was pleased.

"The only thing you really possess is the land and the tribe," the Professor had said. "Everything else is like

*a cloud. You can talk about it if you like, you can
even sit back and look at it, but when you reach for
it, it's not there. What's there is the land, because
when you're gone, it's the greatness of the land that
carries your memory. That's all that history is, the
memory of a tribe. The other thing you got is your
tribe. Your name lives through your tribe. When the
tribe dies, everybody that ever lived in it dies, too.
That's why you got to find a woman who wants to
maintain your tribe. Even if she can't increase it, she's
got to be willing to help nurture and lead it. To let it
suckle at the breasts of her soul."*

Motown felt good. He walked down the street with Didi
and people could see that they were in love. Strangers knew.
If they had known his name, they could have said that he,
Motown, had somebody to love. And who loved him.

Motown had nine dollars, which had to last him another
day, and Didi had more than enough money to get home.
They stopped at a restaurant on Lenox Avenue and ordered
smothered pork chops, collards, and corn bread.

"Have you made love to many girls?" Didi asked.

"I don't remember," Motown said, looking at her.

"Yes, you do," Didi said. "Were they like me?"

"I don't know," Motown said. "Maybe they were only
in my dreams."

"I bet. You know. I really feel good just being able to
say that I love you."

"Makes me feel good saying that I love you," Motown
said.

"You ever say anything on your own?" Didi said, then, thinking that she might have said the wrong thing, put her hand on his. "You say anything you want to say."

"What do you want me to say?"

"What you're thinking?"

"Nothing much." The waitress had brought the orders and carefully set the table, making sure that everything, even the dispenser napkins that she placed under the silverware, were where she wanted them.

"What are you thinking?" Motown asked when the waitress had given the tablecloth a final pat and left.

"That you're very handsome and very nice and very . . . very exciting. I think you're sexy, too."

He listened as she talked, merely playing with her food. He wondered if she could see how much he wanted her. He wondered if his eyes gave him away, or the way he spoke. He wished that he had done something great so that when she wasn't with him, when she was away with her thoughts, she could think about the great thing he had done and it would make him more important to her than leaving Harlem. Perhaps she would think that those things that he thought were important really did matter. Perhaps he could go back to school and learn something, so that when she looked into him with those great eyes of hers she would see something to love. It would be more than him, skulking through shadows or standing in some abandoned hallway with a baseball bat. It would be something wonderful, truly wonderful.

"I'm going to dream about you tonight," she said. "All night long and maybe for the rest of my life."

151:

They kissed on the corner and walked for a while. Then Didi got a cab home. Motown walked, happy and dizzy and laughing his way through the darkening streets.

If any song had all the words to describe how she felt, Didi would have sung it. If any dance had all the steps to capture the lightness she felt, Didi would have danced it. Love played with her as if she was a toy, roughly, gaily, pushing her here and there, making her have to sidestep the people on the sidewalk, making her see miracles where moments before only store fronts had been.

She thought of Motown, how she had resisted him, had fought against loving him. Perhaps she been fighting all the while against loving anyone. Loving had been so hard before Motown.

What she needed was someone to tell. She would tell Tony. She would wake him up and say, "Hey, can you believe it? I'm in love with Motown!"

Tony, of course, wouldn't believe it. He would say that she was grateful, perhaps, or concerned with his safety, but not in love.

"I kept thinking about him," she would say. "I kept thinking about him and picturing him in different ways. I'd picture him going to law school, or to medical school. Once I pictured him in the army. Then I'd picture him the way he is. The way he really is, you know, with that little smile of his digging into you and making you giggle, opening you up when you want to be closed. You know how that is?

"Well," she would say, "I found myself over to his place

doing these little odds and ends for him because I thought he could use it being done, see? And I found myself not wanting to look at his arms because you know I don't go for muscles. What I really want in a guy is someone with a future. But there he stood with all those lean muscles, but not acting like he had them. You know, he never said anything about protecting me or taking care of me and never did anything to really impress me. Of course, helping me out in that fight sure didn't hurt anything, but I mean that he never did anything that was empty. That's what he's about. He doesn't do anything that's empty. Anyway, I ran it through my mind once or twice about how I would be somewhere in some deep trouble and he would come and save me, but it didn't work. Because he's too real to be superman. Then I thought about him being the one to put me in trouble. And I didn't think he would do that but I could picture it and whenever I was around him I felt a little as if I was in danger.

"Tony, what do you think of that?" she would say. And he would say that it was something else, that's what it was. It was something else!

CHAPTER XI

TONY HAD BEEN SO HAPPY WHEN HE HEARD HIS FATHER was coming over. Even though Darlene had told them not to be expecting any big deal, he couldn't help but think it was exactly that, the biggest deal. Didi, with her sassy self, was saying that she wasn't going to do anything special, but then she threw up, which she always did when something big was going on and she wasn't in the center of it. But their father had come drunk. Darlene had cried and said that she didn't want the children to see him that way. He had picked up Didi, held her high over his head, and then put her down.

"You ain't too pretty," he said, "but maybe you gonna be smart."

"Boy, you any kind of man?" he asked, beckoning Tony to him.

"Yeah, I'm a man," he said.

"Yes," Darlene corrected behind him.

His father hit him. He hit him hard. The blow stung the left side of his face and brought tears to his eyes.

"What you hit him like that for?" Darlene's voice split the room in half. "What you hit him like that for?"

"The stuff is weak," Touchy said. "It's some Spanish stuff we been getting lately. It ain't been cut much, it's just weak."

"Then how come the price is the same?" Tony asked.

"The price is the price," Touchy said. "You don't want it, leave it be."

"I'll take it," Tony said.

Tony felt as if he were walking through a hall of mirrors. Everywhere he went he saw himself, sneaking around, looking for something to stick into his veins. It was all he did with his life.

Sometimes, when he got up in the morning, he thought

about playing basketball, but he knew he wouldn't. That was the thing. No matter what he thought about doing he knew that what he would really do is to look for some dope. Now, even after telling Didi how badly he felt, even after looking at himself in the mirror, the tears running down his face and telling himself that he was a junkie and that he needed help, he had sneaked down to the corner and found Touchy and had smiled at him and had given him his mother's money for the dope.

"It ain't been cut much, it's some Spanish stuff."

He knew that Touchy knew about him. He had seen Touchy look at other people posturing before him and had peeped their game. He was a junkie and Touchy knew it and was hard put not to laugh.

Tony dropped his pants and hit the vein in his leg with the back of his middle finger. He snapped at it twice before he saw the blood back up and make the vein bulge slightly. Yes, it was good. He put the stuff that Touchy had sold him in the small pot he had made, that half the kids in the school had made, in shop class by soldering a paper clip onto a bottle cap. Then he put it over the flame until it had liquefied into the cough syrup that he was using. When it was ready, he drew it up into the syringe. He ran the point of the needle over the flame, in the blue part so that it wouldn't get too much carbon on it, and then laying it down, he hit the vein again. He was crying, he felt sorry for himself. It wasn't what he wanted from life. He thought there should be more. Somewhere there should be more. Surely more than Touchy's weak Spanish stuff. Stuff that probably wasn't any more Spanish than Touchy was.

155:

He let a little bit of the almost clear liquid out, seeing that it didn't bubble, then slid the needle easily into his vein. He released the heroin into his leg slowly.

There would be no high. No good feeling. None of it was "good stuff." It would just stop the pain for a few hours, stop the hurting and the frustration. For a few hours it wouldn't hurt at all.

No! It was wrong! The stuff wasn't right! Touchy had said that it was weak, but it wasn't. He felt it deeply, it was like a huge blush gone out of control. He felt it in his fingertips and in his face, around the bridge of his nose. It hadn't been cut at all, not even once.

There was a feeling of panic, as if he was going to release his bowels. He reached for his chest, felt his heart beating. He had been burned! He had used more of it than he should have because Touchy told him it was weak. But it wasn't, or maybe there was something in it. It was definitely wrong!

The street. The thing was to get into the street. Get into the air and burn it off. Go down to the playground and grab a basketball and run and run so that he could burn it off.

Urinate. He thought about urinating. He went into the kitchen and got some water and then went into the bathroom. He stood in front of the toilet and tried to urinate. At first he couldn't, but he felt he had to, it was just a matter of time. Flush it out of his system.

Flush it out and pour some more water on it and flush it some more. Pour some coffee into you. Get that caffeine pumping your heart and getting it through your system. Get down to the court and run around it a few times and make your heart beat and sweat some of it out. Hey, no big deal. Just don't go to sleep, that's all. Turn the water on. Flush it through.

He couldn't urinate. Get some wine. Ain't nothing sweat like a wino. Winos be stinking in the damn hallway, smell like something thrown away. Get out the house. Get out the house. He was scared. Good. Make the heart beat. Pump that stuff through the system. What did the junkie say in the park. Tried to rob a bank when he was high, didn't get no money, lost his buzz. Yeah, lose it.

Got to turn the thing around. No question. Got to turn it around. Touchy's trying to light him up. No, Touchy's done lit him up. There he was, in the hallway now, trying to slide down the wall, trying to slide down the wall without dying before he got to the stairs.

Hey, man, a junkie's supposed to die. You ever see an old junkie? You ever see one of them slick boys popping that bad stuff live more than a few years? Naw, man, them people knowing they dying when they stick that first hit in their arm.

Where was he? At the top of the stairs. It looks so simple when they have junkies on television. Walk around a taste, be cool. Then wait until that next commercial before you be laying up in the bed with everybody standing around telling you how it's going to be all right.

Get down the stairs. The staircase is the longest in the world. There's no air on the staircase. There was nothing except what was suffocating him and falling down on him and sucking out his lungs. Get down the stairs.

Oh my God!

157:

Something's coming. Get down the stairs before it gets to you, man. Get down the stairs! Jump down the stairs. Fall down the stairs. It's coming, man, and it's mean. It's so damn mean.

Oh my God!

I'm so sorry. I'm so sorry. Get up! Get up from here and get some air. Stick your head out the window. Break a window. Can't see anything. Can't see anything. Maybe I'll be all right. Maybe I'll be all right. When all this is over and I come out from where I am, maybe I'll be all right. Then I'll get straight. That's stone the word.

Didi?

Mama?

Mama?

Oh my God!

CHAPTER

"WHY DO I HAVE TO GO DOWN TO SOMEPLACE TO SEE him?" Didi was wild-eyed and wild-haired and possessed with the demon of her fury. "Why! Why!"

"It's a formality, miss," the police officer said. "Someone from the family has to identify the deceased. Your mother's in no shape. I know it's hard but—"

"How do you know?" Didi screamed at him. "How do you know?"

"I've seen enough pain to recognize it," he said. "I see

it up here every day. I'm not asking you to come down, I'm just telling you what the procedure is."

That's what the conversation with the policeman was.

"Didi, I know how you feel, but you have to stay with your mother. Child, you the one that's carrying on and she's just sitting there rockin' but she bleeding more than you know how to bleed. She's the boy's mother. Now you got to stay with her."

That's how the conversation with the neighbor went.

"Somebody go with her before she hurt herself," the high-pitched, anonymous voice came from the crowd. "And somebody else go up to the place so them policemans don't steal nothing."

"Motown," she would say. "I got somebody for you to kill. The fool's name is Touchy."

CHAPTER XIII

ALL OF HIS LIFE MOTOWN HAD LIVED FOR JUST SUCH A moment. It would be a moment of greatness. A moment in which he would make up for all the years of being nothing, of being without friends or family. Some moment would come along and he would rise to it and be the hero. Eyes would turn his way. People seeing him would wave and point him out to their children. A woman, his woman, would look at him with pride and love in her eyes.

Often he would dream of such moments. There would

be a life to be saved, a battle to be won, a plan needed to save the world. And always, in his dream, he would reach for the moment, the greatness.

But this was no dream. This was a real thing, a thing to be felt, to be touched. Her name was Didi.

This was Didi, who filled his head even more than the Professor did. Didi, who could hold him close and murmur "Oh, baby" as she lay against his chest rearranging the firmness of his flesh and of his bones. It was Didi who brought the moment to life.

Didi.

"Tony's dead," she had said. Fierce-eyed, a nightmare she-wolf, a stranger, a banshee come screaming from the streets to stand in the hallway of the first apartment he had ever had in his entire life.

"What happened?" he had asked, his heart breaking to feel her pain.

"He died from the dope." She looked up at him, searched his eyes. Searched his thoughts. Searched back to the mama he didn't remember and the father he had tried so hard to forget.

"Didi," her name came out slowly. Motown sensed that she would explode. Sensed it and wanted to grab her before it was too late.

"I want you to kill him," she said. Her nose was running. She was crying. "You got to kill him. He killed my brother!"

"Touchy?"

"I hate him!" she screamed. She picked up a magazine and threw it across the room. "I hate him!"

"The dope is eating at the tribe. It's eating at it the same way that a cancer eats at the body. You got to know who your enemy is," the Professor had said. "Anybody who brings dope into the tribe is your enemy. They're killing the tribe as sure as cancer. Sucking its life out and leaving zombies in the street."

"Didi, maybe we should go to the police." Motown's words echoed in his head.

"How *can* we? How *can* we?" She looked at him as if she didn't know him, not knowing that even as she looked at him, he was wondering who she was.

"We just can't . . . you know." He looked away.

"Don't look away from me!" she called to him. "Don't look away from me!"

"You want me to kill him?"

"I want you to—I want you to show me who you are, I want you to show me . . ." She slumped down on the chair. Then she looked up, slowly. "I'll do it myself."

"No." Motown put his hand on her as she reached for the steak knife that she had brought for him. "You stay here. I'll get him."

Motown took the money he had to get to work the next day. He already had his sneakers on and he changed from a shirt with a collar to a soft beige tee shirt. Didi was lying on the bed, her shoulders lifting and falling with her sobs.

It was hard, life in Harlem, and Didi couldn't take it. It was too much for her. She wasn't meant for this kind of life. She wasn't meant for these times and this place. Hers was a different world from his, but he would always be with her somehow. Now, in this time when someone had to speak about how the tribe should be, and how a man had to be with a woman, Motown would lift his voice, and his arm. It would be his gift.

The stores in Harlem sell whatever they can. Sometimes they just sell food and a few things like playing cards and dice in cellophane wrappers. Sometimes they sold dream books next to crucifixes and tennis balls next to roach poisons. Anything a person needed that the cops wouldn't stop them from selling was fair game. Most of the small variety shops sold at least one kind of knife.

"This little baby here costs five dollars and it'll stay sharp about as long as you want it to." The brother behind the counter was wearing green pants, a green shirt, two gold chains, and sneakers. "Good for all kinds of things. You can even cut linoleum up with this thing."

"I ain't got but three dollars," Motown said.

"Then take this Japanese knife," the brother said. "All you got to do is to sharpen it once or twice a month and it's just as good as that other knife. That other knife got Swedish steel and that's the best there is. But this knife is cool, too."

Motown paid the three dollars, opened the knife and closed it twice to get the feel of it, and put it in his pocket. He tried not to think about killing Touchy, or about what would happen after he had.

You have to bring your nose to flowers but bad news travels like stink on the wind. They arrested nine junkies when they found Anthony had overdosed. They got one from every block from 126th through 129th and the rest they got in one bunch as they were sitting in front of the New Hope Baptist Church eating mangoes. Reese the undertaker told the Professor that they were rounding up junkies and that there was a panic on the street.

"They scared their stuff gonna be off the street for a few hours," Reese said, his gold tooth showing as he spoke.

The Professor didn't pay any mind to it. They had rounded up junkies before. Once when Carter had come to Harlem, they had rounded up over fifty junkies to get them off the street. They even got one guy who worked downtown in a bakery and just looked like he was sleepy on the way home. It was all window dressing, all show, the Professor knew, and it was not his concern. At least it wasn't until Tutmose came and asked him if he had heard the news.

"I heard they're arresting a few victims," the Professor said. "Putting the junkies in jail."

"No, that ain't what I mean. You know Didi? That girl that Motown be liking?"

"Yes."

"Well, her brother died. They say that's why they picking up all the heads."

No one knew how much money the Professor had. He had saved and pushed and tucked and scrimped over the years until he had accumulated nearly seven thousand dollars. It wasn't a large amount according to some standards, but it was something. For a black man, it could be a whole lot of something. He had been thinking about the money. He really didn't need it. He owned the little book store that he ran and the building it was in. He wouldn't get more than a thousand dollars or so for it if he tried to sell it, but as long as he had it, he would always have a roof over his head. He didn't eat much and what little he did eat his social security pension would take care of. He hadn't wanted to pay social security all the years he had worked in the garment center but now he was glad, the money gave him dignity. It might not have been a lot of dignity, but it was enough.

He had been thinking about Motown for a long time. The boy needed a break. He needed someone to give him a leg up, but the Professor had held back. The boy was doing too good on his own. True, he wasn't living high, but he was living within himself. He was a black man-child coming into his own. The Professor had thought about giving the money to Motown, telling him to take it and make a life for himself, to use it to learn and to use what he had learned for the tribe. When Tutmose told him that Anthony had died, he felt a pain somewhere deep in his bowels. Motown, he knew, could only take so much. He had seen other good young men eroded by the grind of the hard streets, worn down by too many battles. Now was the time to give the boy the money. He had thought about leaving it to him once, but who knew when that might be. Who knew when death would claim him. No, now was the time, before the world pressed too hard on him.

He closed the shop in the middle of the day for the first time in thirty years. The thought of someone coming and looking in, wanting a book and not being able to get it bothered him, but only for a moment. They weren't hungry for books these days. They had fallen off from knowing, had been tricked into a life of senses, of feeling relief from pain and calling it good.

The Professor had already walked past Motown's house. He wanted to know where the boy stayed. Wanted to know if he had a good place, a safe place.

He would go get him and sit him down and talk to him. Take him off into the dark hut of his mind and cut away the ties to his boyhood, heal him with the ashes of his words and let Motown, the man, emerge. It was time.

He felt a sense of urgency. He felt a sense of wanting to hurry and of worrying whether he should have done it a year before, perhaps a week, perhaps a day.

There was joy to it, too. What greater joy than to see a boy become a man?

"You can't play no checkers!" A man railed at an old lady, the two of them sitting on wooden chairs in front of a record shop, the small loud speaker dangling from a wire above them blaring out gospel music.

Je-sus lo . . . ver of my soul . . .

The old woman put her fingers, black and thin, over the checker and picked it up.

"Uh! Uh! Uh!" She grunted as she jumped her opponent's last three men. Then, with a sweep of her hand, she swept the checkers off the board onto the sidewalk.

The Professor reached Motown's house and sat on the steps. His breath didn't come the way it had once when he would go to the YMCA on 135th and swim until his shoulders ached. His heart was a drum in his throat now, warning him when the flesh was weakening, the pace too quick. He sat on the steps for a moment, rolling the words about in his mind. He wouldn't want the boy to feel as if he was giving him charity. It was responsibility that he was offering. That and the years of his own sweat.

Rested, he went up the steps of the brownstone and rang the bell. He waited. Suppose the boy wasn't home? Then he would wait for him. Even he had that much time. He rang the bell again, surprised at his own impatience. The buzzer rang and he pushed the door open. He went in. There were good smells. Curried plantains frying on the first floor, on the second, perfume.

The door opened and the girl looked at him. Her hair formed a dark halo around her pretty face. She was tall, with good bones, he thought. They looked well together.

"Oh, hello," she said. She stood away from the door. She smiled but her face was troubled. Her eyes, normally wide with youth, were narrowed and glistening with tears. He put his hand on hers and squeezed it gently.

"I'm sorry," he said.

She nodded and sat down at the table. He didn't see the boy. Had he gone out?

"Is there anything I can do?" the Professor asked.

"No," she said, forcing a smile through her tears. How pretty she was. If it had been another time and another place, he would have sat at her side, the elder offering his advice to the young queen. Now he sat across from her, too many worlds apart to reach her.

The moments fell between them slowly. The feeling of

urgency had returned. He could feel his chest tighten. Was it something to concern him, or just the pull of the stairs on an old man?

"Where is Motown?" he asked.

"He went to get Touchy," she said.

"Touchy?"

"The one that killed my brother," she said. Her lips tightened unevenly, allowing the teeth on one side of her mouth to show in an angry snarl. "He's going to kill him."

He stood quickly. His mouth opened but the lips that moved were silent. His mind raced to the streets. There was Motown, chest bared, what would he have? A knife? A gun? The strength of his own black hands?

"This was his idea?" he asked, trying to keep the pain from his voice.

She looked up at him, her eyes growing wider. She looked into his face searching for his meaning.

"What?" she asked.

"This inviting death to dance," the Professor said. "It was the boy's idea."

"Somebody . . ." She stood and turned to the wall, bringing her hand to her face.

"Somebody must do something?" he asked, touching her elbow. "True, but is it his idea to do this foolish thing? To throw his life away after what is already gone?"

"What difference does it make whose idea it is?" Didi turned to him. "You live with your ideas about what happened a thousand years ago in Africa, I have to live now. Don't you understand that? Is that so . . ."

She was trembling in her fury, and her pain and her frustration. She trembled, shook, until her body released the sobs that it could barely contain.

The sound of her crying filled the room. Filled every dark corner, pushed against the peeling plaster, found the crevices in the floor, made the light string sway, rattled the windows.

"What you feel is true," he said, turning the doorknob. "But what will we live with if we let our young men die? What will we have to live with?"

She couldn't hear him and he had no time to wait for her.

"Where is this Touchy?" He shook her arm, gently at first, then harder. "Tell me where he is. Where will Motown find him? Where will he look?"

She turned away.

"Child, please . . ."

The Professor stood, naked in his old age, his lined face filled with the worries of his heart, talking to her quietly. His hand, the nails rounded and yellowed with age, touched her shoulder cautiously, as if he could, by doing so, form some bridge between them. But even his deep care was no match for her anger and he could only plead with hopeful eyes and a tired voice.

"Child, please . . ."

He wanted to save Motown. He was begging her to help him. His hand touched her again, tentatively. His voice was so calm and yet she knew the turmoil that he felt. She felt it herself.

She pictured Motown confronting Touchy in the street. Motown would move quickly, grabbing Touchy by the throat. Maybe he would kill him. What would happen then? Would she go to the police and say that it was right? Would she say that they couldn't do their job and so she had called upon Motown's love for her to do it for them?

"Child, please . . ."

"What shall I do?" she asked the Professor.

"Come with me," he said. "Show me the way. There might still be time."

CHAPTER XIV

WHAT WAS HARLEM? A PLACE, A NAME, A GAUDY EASEL OF colors that they rushed by as they plummeted their way through the streets. Frantically they stood on the corner as people watched them, put down their numbers slips, their dominoes, their burdens for a moment.

"He got him something young and he's in a hurry to get at it before he die," a youngblood said.

"Naw." This from an older man, already grayed at the temples, most of his teeth missing. "They got the troubles bad, them two."

Others turned and saw them, a young black girl, taller than most, her body young and alive, her round thighs filling the jeans she wore, her feet impatiently quick on the hot asphalt. And he, an old man with a tired body, but eyes quicker than the girl's feet, with a mind racing faster than his flesh had ever carried him. They stood waving in the street until a gypsy cab pulled up in front of them. He let the girl in first.

She was in and pulling him in.

"What have I done?" She looked at the Professor, her face twisted with despair. "I don't want to throw Motown's life away, too."

"Give the man the address," he said, holding her together with the evenness of his words.

"A Hundred Thirty-third and Lexington," she said. "Please hurry."

"I love him," she said. "I love him."

"I know," the Professor said. "I know about love."

Who else would you ask to give up their life except a lover, he asked himself.

Two young boys, one carrying a radio strolled in front of the cab, stopped to have a conversation, making the cab wait.

"Please," the Professor said, "a young man is in trouble."

"I'll be in trouble, too, if I mess with these bloods," the driver said. "Don't say nothing to them, and they'll get on the way."

The girl was holding together better now. She was pulling herself together. She was reaching down somewhere through the eddy of grief and pain and was finding strength. How strong his people were. How strong they were. They would prevail. It was a matter of time, and of finding the right young people to take the front ranks.

"Down this street!"

The cab driver made a sharp turn and then brought the cab to a quick halt.

"There's something going on down there," he said. "I ain't got no insurance for this car so you got to get out here."

"There's a young black man in trouble," the Professor said. "Will you deny him?"

"Look, man," the driver turned around. He had a gold tooth in the front of his mouth.

"Move it!" Didi's voice startled the Professor. He looked at her. There was fury in her eyes. Her neck was stretched tight, the skin on her face drawn back.

The driver turned and started the cab. In a second they were on the crowd, scattering bodies.

In the distance the wail of a police car grew louder.

"Here comes the police," a fat yellowish woman with too much makeup called out. "Go on and get it on if you got the heart!"

"Burn him, Carlos!" Touchy took advantage of the distraction to shout at his man.

Touchy saw Carlos's eyes flicker nervously over the crowd that seemed to grow larger every moment, stop for a moment on Motown's coiled form, and then lower the gun to the fender of the car and push it toward him.

"You want him," Carlos said, "you get him!"

Touchy grabbed the gun. Motown was crazy. That's what was wrong with him. He had to get him. He lifted the gun as Motown, his face glistening with sweat, brought the knife back and started wildly across the street.

"Motown!" It was the girl, to his left, screaming, her arms high as she neared him. Touchy felt the gun jerk in his hand as he pulled the trigger.

The girl flying toward him, her arms high, now spinning, her legs coming out from under her—a bird shot down in mid-flight. Touchy brought his arm up just in time to catch Motown's arm. He felt himself going down under its strength. He tried to catch himself as he slid along the fender of the car. He hit the ground hard, with Motown on top of him. Motown put his knee on Touchy's arm, pinning it to the ground. The edge of the knife caught the sun as Motown lifted it above his head.

Another scream, higher than the first, a chilling scream that Touchy turned away from. Then another form above him, leaping onto the boy, bringing the blade crashing into the side of the car. Both of them were above him now, pinning him to the street. The boy's face an Ashanti mask, the girl wild-eyed, fierce.

"No, baby, don't!" the girl was yelling into Motown's face.

Touchy tried to free his arm. Motown put his hand on Touchy's neck and leaned forward, putting his weight on his extended arm. Touchy gasped for breath as the girl jerked the gun from his hand and sent it skidding under the car.

Motown felt confused as someone pulled him up. He looked up to see Tutmose and felt his friend's hands tremble on his arms. Around them, suddenly, were policemen. Some were in uniform, others in civilian dress with badges pinned to their jackets.

"He the one!" An old West Indian lady with hips wide enough to rock the world pointed at where Touchy still lay half under the car. "He the one shot that girl!"

Motown jerked his head around, looking for Didi. She stood leaning against a lamppost. There was blood on her jeans, blood streaked down her arm.

"Didi?" He looked at her. Searched her eyes. Crossed to her. Touched her shoulder with his fingertips. "Didi?"

"I'm okay," she said, smiling through tears.

Motown looked at the blood and turned back to where two policemen were pushing a handcuffed Touchy into a patrol car. Rage swelled his chest as he saw him.

"No, son." The Professor was at his side. "Don't give yourself up, you were meant for better than this."

The overhead lights on the patrol car began to turn and the car moved quickly toward Lenox Avenue.

The crowd didn't disperse. What else was there to do on the hot Harlem streets except to watch what happens and, later, to relive it on the streets and in the bodegas? A policeman looked at Didi's arm and said he thought it wasn't too bad. He called over the attendant from the orange and white city ambulance that had bullied its way through the onlookers.

"It ain't that bad," the long-headed attendant said. "She got to have it treated but it didn't get no bone or nothing. She'll be okay. My man here look worse than she do."

Motown turned to where the Professor stood, his chest still heaving from his efforts, his face full, almost gray.

"Professor, you okay?"

"I'm okay," the Professor said. "More than I've been in

a while. Just tired, that's all. You go on with the girl to the hospital. When you get back to the tribe I'll be waiting. Then we'll have tea and we'll talk."

Motown got into the ambulance with Didi. The driver closed the doors, shutting out the noises and the life that filled the streets. Motown took Didi's hand.

"Does it hurt much?"

"Not if you love me," she said.

He had thought, for some reason, that he had pulled himself together. Thought that the steel that he had forged in the streets and in the darkness of the buildings and in the solitude of his own soul had again hardened. Motown had something to say, something about loving her, but when he looked into Didi's face he couldn't form the words that welled in his throat. Gently he took her hand and held it against his cheek, and gently turned it in his own hands, hands that would have killed for her, but now would work for her and protect her, and gently he brought her hand to his lips and kissed it. Again he tried to speak, to tell her what he felt, and again nothing came from his trembling lips. Didi pulled his head to her lips and kissed away the tears.

"I know, sweetness," she said softly. "I know."

About the Author

Walter Dean Myers has written many novels for young adults, including two ALA Notable Books, *Fast Sam, Cool Clyde, and Stuff* and *It Ain't All for Nothin'*, and two ALA Best Books for Young Adults, *The Young Landlords* and *The Legend of Tarik*. Mr. Myers lives in New Jersey.